"I Thought You Said You Were A *Reformed* Rake."

Sam's lips curved into a grin. "Even a reformed rake slips now and again." Cupping a hand at her cheek, he touched his lips to her, withdrew with a low hum of pleasure, then returned for a second taste.

"Sweet," he murmured, tracing his tongue along her lower lip. Angling his body more fully toward hers, he pushed his fingers through her hair and took the kiss deeper.

God help me, she thought weakly. Though every nerve in her body demanded she respond, intellectually she knew what a mistake that would be. Any kind of intimacy, no matter how innocent, could jeopardize their business relationship.

If that wasn't reason enough for her to put an end to this foolishness, he was a virtual stranger. She didn't know him. Not in the sense a woman needed to know a man before making love to him.

Yet in spite of the reasons pointing her away from Sam, she found herself melting against him, until every thought leaked from her mind, save one. Him.

Dear Reader,

Sometimes life is stranger than fiction. From the moment I decided to write this series, focusing on the lives of six fictional Vietnam soldiers, my husband and I have experienced several real-life encounters that seemed to hauntingly parallel the events of the book I was writing at that particular moment. This book was no exception.

In this story, the soldier mentioned in the prologue is listed as MIA (Missing In Action). That, in itself, isn't strange, as the list of MIA's is, sadly, very long. What *is* strange is that while at a cocktail party, my husband and I were visiting with several of the guests and the topic somehow segued to tattoos. Several of the men had tattoos, including my husband, and all confessed that they had gotten them while serving in Vietnam. From there, the conversation drifted to what branch of the service each served in. When my husband told the group that he was a Green Beret, one of the guests said that her son-in-law's father was a Green Beret, too, and was still listed as MIA. Curious to discover if he had known her relative, my husband asked the soldier's name…and this is where the "life is stranger than fiction" phenomenon steps in. Not only did my husband *know* her relative, he served in the same unit with him in Vietnam.

In spite of all the stranger-than-life encounters that have occurred during the writing of this series, all of the characters and the stories I've created around their lives are entirely fictional…but who knows? Maybe there is a soldier somewhere out there who wanted his story told and used me as his medium. Like I said, life is sometimes stranger than fiction.

Peggy Moreland

PEGGY MORELAND

THE TEXAN'S HONOR-BOUND PROMISE

Published by Silhouette Books
America's Publisher of Contemporary Romance

SILHOUETTE BOOKS

ISBN-13: 978-0-373-76750-2
ISBN-10:   0-373-76750-1

THE TEXAN'S HONOR-BOUND PROMISE

Copyright © 2006 by Peggy Bozeman Morse

This edition published by arrangement with Harlequin Books S.A.

® and TM are trademarks of Harlequin Books S.A., used under license. Trademarks indicated with ® are registered in the United States Patent and Trademark Office, the Canadian Trade Marks Office and in other countries.

Visit Silhouette Books at www.eHarlequin.com

Printed in U.S.A.

Recent books by Peggy Moreland

Silhouette Desire

*Five Brothers and a Baby #1532
*Baby, You're Mine #1544
*The Last Good Man in Texas #1580
*Sins of a Tanner #1616
*Tanner Ties #1676
†The Texan's Forbidden Affair #1718
†The Texan's Convenient Marriage #1736
†The Texan's Honor-Bound Promise #1750

Silhouette Books

*Tanner's Millions

*The Tanners of Texas
†A Piece of Texas

PEGGY MORELAND

published her first romance with Silhouette Books in 1989, and continues to delight readers with stories set in her home state of Texas. Winner of the National Readers' Choice Award, a nominee for *Romantic Times BOOKclub* Reviewer's Choice Award and a two-time finalist for the prestigious RITA® Award, Peggy's books frequently appear on the *USA TODAY* and Waldenbooks bestseller lists. When not writing, you can usually find Peggy outside, tending the cattle, goats and other critters on the ranch she shares with her husband. You may write to Peggy at P.O. Box 1099, Florence, TX 76527-1099, or e-mail her at peggy@peggymoreland.com.

This book is dedicated to all the wives, children and families of soldiers listed as Missing In Action while in the service of our country.

Prologue

I can't promise you that I will bring you all home alive. But this I swear before you and before Almighty God: that when we go into battle, I will be the first to set foot on the field and I will be the last to step off and I will leave no one behind. Dead or alive, we will all come home together. So help me God.

—Lt. Colonel Hal Moore
(from the movie *We Were Soldiers*)

July, 1972

The mood around camp was subdued. Those soldiers who had ventured from their sleeping quarters sat in silence, their heads down, their expressions somber, their thoughts focused on the previous day's events and their chances of making it home alive. For some, this war was a joke, a part in an elaborate play they acted out each day, under the direction of their supervising officer.

Not so for Jessie Kittrell.

To Jessie—or T.J., as he was called by his friends—this war was his one chance to escape poverty, to give his family the kind of life he'd never known. With a wife and child to support and another baby on the way, enlisting in the army had seemed the only way out of the financial rut he was trapped in. Besides the training it provided, once he fulfilled his years of service, the army would pay for his college education, courtesy of the GI Bill.

If he survived this hell, he thought grimly. Like most of the men he fought alongside, before arriving in Vietnam, he hadn't given survival much thought. He'd been too caught up in the we're-gonna-whip-some-butts mentality ingrained in them all during boot camp. He'd carried that cockiness with him into his first battle…and left it there, along with the contents of his stomach.

Desperate to block the images that pushed into his mind, he reached inside his shirt pocket for the photo he kept close to his heart. Dirty and creased from frequent handling, the photo was his anchor, his reminder of what he fought for, his reason for being here, his need to survive.

Tears burned behind his eyes as he stared down at his wife and daughter. God, he missed them. Three months was a long time for a man to go without seeing his family. Leah had turned two last week, a birthday party he'd missed. Would she remember him when he returned home? Would she wrap her arms around his neck and plaster a wet kiss on his cheek when she saw him, as she had in the past? Or would she cringe away and cry for her mommy?

The dull *whop-whop-whop* of helicopter blades overhead had him looking up. Knowing the chopper's purpose, he slowly tucked the picture back into his pocket. He watched silently as the Huey landed and two bagged bodies were loaded onto the deck. He gulped back emotion, aware that a third soldier should have been making that ride. Buddy Crandall.

But Buddy wouldn't be making the trip back home.

A wide hand landed on his shoulder and he glanced up to find Pops—the nickname given Larry Blair by T.J. and the rest of the guys—beside him, his gaze on the helicopter as the pilot prepared to take off.

"It's not right," T.J. said, shaking his head. "Buddy should be on that chopper."

"Yeah," Pops said quietly. "But some things just aren't meant to be."

"MIA," T.J. muttered, squinting his eyes as he watched the helicopter slowly rise into the air. "Can you imagine what getting that news is going to do to Buddy's family? Why can't the Army list him as Killed in Action rather than Missing in Action? Hell, we all know he's dead! We were there. We saw what happened. There's no way he made it out of there alive."

"You know the rules," Pops reminded him gently. "If a soldier's body isn't recovered and his death not positively verified, he's MIA."

"I don't want my family put through that," T.J. said furiously. He glanced up at Pops. "Promise me something, Pops."

"If I can."

"If what happened to Buddy should happen to me, promise me you'll let my family know. Tell 'em I fought and died like a solider. Tell 'em I won't be coming home."

Pops hesitated a moment, then nodded soberly. "Consider it done." He gave T.J.'s shoulder a comforting squeeze. "Check your gear. We'll be pulling out in a couple of hours."

T.J. sat a moment longer, then dragged a hand across the moisture in his eyes and stood. He patted his pocket and the photo he kept there, then strode for his tent and the pack that held his gear.

One

The Craftsman-style two-story house Sam parked his truck in front of was situated in an older neighborhood near Tyler, Texas's downtown area. A breezeway connected the house to a carriage-style garage and served as a pass-through to the garage's rear entrance, discreetly hidden in the backyard.

The house was owned by Leah Kittrell. Mack McGruder had provided Sam with the woman's name, as well as her address and telephone number. An Internet search had provided him with a few more details. According to the information he'd found, Ms. Kittrell owned her own business—Stylized Events—had gone through a messy divorce three years prior and currently served on the boards of several civic and charity organizations. The photos he'd found of her in the archive section on the Tyler newspaper's Web site provided an image of a woman who appeared to be in her late twenties to early thirties, with long dark hair, classic features and legs that seemed to stretch forever.

More facts than he probably needed, but Sam preferred to know as much about a person as he could before entering into negotiations.

Now all he had to do was squeeze what he wanted out of the woman and he could call it a day.

Confident that he'd be back on the road within the hour, he punched the doorbell, then stepped back, smoothing a hand over hair the wind had rumpled earlier while he was changing a flat tire on the interstate.

The door swung open and a woman appeared. Leah Kittrell, he thought, easily recognizing her from the photos he'd found on the internet. But the pictures hadn't done her justice, he thought appreciatively. While attractive in the photographs, in person she was drop-dead gorgeous. What the pictures had revealed as dark hair was in fact a sleek raven-black. But the image of her legs had been right on target. They did seem to stretch forever.

Mesmerized by eyes the color of aged whiskey, it took him a moment to realize that she was frowning at him. He quickly extended his hand.

"Sam Forrester," he said, introducing himself.

She glanced down at the hand he offered and her frown deepened. Following her gaze, he saw the grease that stained his palm and yanked it back to drag across the seat of his jeans. "Sorry. Had a blowout on the way here. Haven't had a chance to clean up."

Her gaze met his again. "How many are you expecting for dinner?"

He blinked. Blinked again. "Excuse me?"

Rolling her eyes, she angled her head and pointed to the minuscule headset attached to her ear.

"Oh," he murmured, realizing that her question hadn't been directed to him but someone she was talking to on her cellular phone. "Sorry."

She stepped back and motioned for him to come inside. "Forty guests," she said thoughtfully as she closed the door behind him. "To be safe, I'd suggest we plan to serve thirty-five. Some won't bother to RSVP but will come anyway. Others will say they're coming and not show up."

She turned for the rear of the house, curling her finger in a signal for him to follow. With a shrug, he trailed behind her, glancing at the rooms they passed through. Neat as a pin, he noted. Not a thing out of place. Not even in the kitchen. The woman either had a full-time housekeeper or was anal as hell.

She opened a rear door, stepped out onto a patio and led the way to the garage. *It's in there,* she mouthed, indicating a side door.

Wondering what "it" was, he eased past her and opened the door. Like the rest of her house, the garage was hospital-clean and neat as a pin. An SUV was parked in the slot nearest him. In the other, a vintage Ford Mustang.

He pressed a hand over his heart. "Oh, man," he murmured and headed for it.

He walked a slow circle around the car, then stopped in front and popped the hood. Behind him he could hear Leah talking on the phone, but he was more interested in the vintage set of wheels in front of him than her discussion of food and flowers.

Bracing a hand on the radiator for support, he stuck his head beneath the hood in order to check out the engine. "Two hundred and fifty ponies," he said with a lustful sigh.

"So? What do you think?"

He jumped at the sound of her voice and bumped his head on the hood. Muttering a curse, he straightened, rubbing a hand over his head.

She winced. "Ouch. Bet that hurt."

Grimacing, he dropped his hand. "I've had worse." He turned back to the car and lowered the hood. "Sorry for being nosy, but I couldn't resist. Is it yours?"

"My brother's," she replied, then amended, "Or it was."

He glanced back, a brow lifted in question.

"He was killed in Iraq about six months ago. He promised my nephew, Craig, he could have the car when he turned sixteen. They were going to start restoring it when my brother returned from Iraq." She glanced at the car, drew in a steadying breath. When she faced him again, her jaw was set in determination. "I intend to see that at least part of his promise is kept, which is why I advertised for a mechanic to do the restoration."

And she thought he was a mechanic who'd come in response to her ad, Sam deduced. Though he knew he should correct her mistake, he decided, for the moment at least, to keep the purpose of his visit to himself and said instead, "I'm sorry for your loss."

"*I'm* sorry he ever enlisted."

Surprised by the bitterness in her voice, he began to circle the car again. "How long had he owned it?" he asked curiously.

"Forever."

He shot her a glance over the roof of the car and she shrugged. "My father was the original owner. I guess you could say Kevin inherited it from him."

He turned his gaze back to the car and saw the Army decal on the rear window, it's edges curled and brittle, and knew, by its age, her father was the one who had put it there, not her brother. Thinking this might be the opening he needed, he asked, "Your father was in the Army, too?"

She followed his gaze to the decal. "MIA, Vietnam."

"Your family made a considerable sacrifice for our country."

She flattened her lips. "Not by choice, I assure you." She flapped a hand, dismissing the subject, then glanced at her watch. "My nephew should be here soon. He wants to help with the restoration. Do you have a problem with that?"

Again he felt he should correct her mistake and tell her the true purpose of his visit. But he had a feeling if he did, she'd toss him out on his ear.

"Can't see why I would," he replied vaguely.

She smiled, seemingly relieved by his response. "Good. Craig really needs this."

Before he could ask her what she meant by the statement, the door opened and a young voice called, "Aunt Leah? You in here?"

Leah turned, her smile widening. "Come on in and join us, Craig. How was school?"

Head down, a boy—somewhere between twelve and fourteen, judging by his size—shuffled toward them, one hand cinched around the strap of a backpack he had draped over his shoulder, the other stuffed in the pocket of jeans at least a size too large for his thin frame. "Okay, I guess."

Sam yearned for a pair of scissors so that he could whack off enough of the kid's hair to see his face.

"Craig, I'd like you to meet—" She stopped short, then looked at Sam in embarrassment. "I'm sorry. I can't remember your name."

"Sam Forrester."

Smiling, she extended her hand. "Leah Kittrell."

He held up his palm, reminding her of the grease that stained it.

She tucked her hand behind her back. "Uh, right." She turned to her nephew and, smiling again, wrapped an arm around his shoulders and drew him to her side. "Sam, this is my nephew, Craig. Craig, Mr. Forrester."

"Sam will do," Sam offered, then smiled at the kid. "Nice to meet you, Craig."

Craig mumbled a barely audible, "Yeah. You, too."

"Sam is here to discuss restoring the car," she told her nephew.

He glanced up at Sam through the mass of bangs he hid behind, then dropped his gaze and turned away with a mumbled "Whatever" and headed back toward the house.

"Hey!" Leah called after him. "Where are you going?"

"Homework."

"But don't you want—"

The door slammed, cutting her off. Heaving a sigh, she turned and gave Sam an apologetic smile. "He really is a nice kid. He's just been having a tough time. Losing his father hit him pretty hard."

"Tough blow for a kid his age."

"Yes, it is."

He frowned, remembering the boy's reference to homework, as well as her mention earlier about school. "Isn't school out for the summer?"

"For most students. Craig failed two classes, so he has to go to summer school."

He nodded, wondering if the kid's father's death had anything to do with his failure.

She opened her hands. "So? What do you think? Are you interested in the job?"

You've really stepped in it now, Sam thought, realizing too late his mistake in allowing her to go on believing he was a mechanic. He supposed he could tell her the restoration would take more work than he'd first thought and make a fast exit.

But that would mean leaving without getting the information he'd promised Mack, which didn't settle well with him at all. He owed Mack. Bigtime. And he was determined to honor that debt.

Pursing his lips thoughtfully, he studied the car as if considering whether or not he wanted to take on the job while buying himself some time to figure out what he should do.

Getting the information for Mack wasn't going to be the easy-in-easy-out mission he'd first thought. Mack had warned him about Leah's obstinance in refusing to discuss her father, but Sam hadn't taken him seriously until he'd gotten a taste of it himself.

It was going to take some time to finesse her into telling him what he wanted to know.

And restoring the car might be just the ploy he needed to gain that time.

But if he agreed to work on the car, he'd be saddling himself with a troubled teen. Sam had seen the resentment, as well as the grief, that shadowed the boy's eyes and suspected it was the loss of his father that had put them both there. Sam had lost a father, too, at a fairly young age. Not to death, but a loss just the same, and he understood what the boy was going through…and where he'd end up if someone didn't intervene.

He had a month, he reminded himself, with nothing to do but puzzle out the direction he wanted to point his future in. He could think as easily working on a car as he could lying on his back on some sun-drenched beach surrounded by bikini-clad women.

Decided, he said to Leah, "Yeah, I'm interested."

He would swear he felt her sigh of relief from five feet away.

"I have no idea what kind of payment to offer you. I know nothing about this kind of thing or how long it would take to complete the job. I guess it would simplify matters if you'd simply tell me what you'd charge for the restoration, then I could determine whether or not I can afford to hire you."

"Since you want your nephew to help with the restoration, I suppose the work will need to be done here?"

"That would be best. He comes here after school each day."

Nodding, he began to circle the car again. "I've only got a month to devote to the job, but I think I could get it done in that length of time. Most of it, anyway."

"Are you saying you'll do it?"

Smiling, he stroked a hand over the Mustang emblem on the hood. "Hard to say no to a beauty like this."

"We haven't decided on a fee yet," she reminded him.

He hitched his hands on his hips and looked up at the ceiling. "Most carriage houses like this have an apartment overhead. Does this one?"

"W-well, yes," she stammered as if wondering why he'd ask. "Although not a full one. Just a bedroom, sitting room and bath."

Lowering his chin, he met her gaze. "Tell you what. Provide me with room and board for the next month, and we'll call it even."

"Room and board?" she repeated dully.

"I'm not from around here. In order to do the work, I'd need a place to stay."

She nervously wet her lips. "I suppose that would be okay. The apartment's furnished. I keep it ready for relatives and friends who come to visit. But I don't cook," she was quick to inform him. "Not regularly, at any rate."

"As long as I'm allowed access to your kitchen, I can see to my own meals."

She eyed him suspiciously. "And that's all you want in exchange for doing the work? Room and board?"

He hid a smile. "If you're worried I'll demand sexual favors, I won't." He waited a beat, then added, "Although I wouldn't turn them down if offered."

She jutted her chin. "I'll want references."

He shrugged. "Fine with me. None will be local, though. Lampasas is where I call home."

Her brows shot high. "How on earth did you hear about the ad I placed? Lampasas is hours from here."

He shot her a wink. "I guess some things were just meant to be."

As he pulled away from Leah's house, Sam punched in Mack's phone number. His friend answered on the first ring, obviously awaiting the call.

"Did you talk to her?" Mack asked anxiously.

"I did," Sam replied. "And the answer to your next question is no. I haven't gotten the information you need. But I'm working on it, which is why I called. I need a favor."

"What?"

"Personal references."

"Why?"

"I'll explain later. Right now I need you to call Lenny, Pastor Nolan, Bill and Jack Phelps. Tell them that Leah Kittrell might be calling and asking questions about me. If she does, tell them to keep whatever information they offer to a minimum and not to mention anything about me being in the Army."

"Why not?" Mack asked in confusion. "Your service record is nothing to be ashamed of."

"No," Sam agreed. "But if Leah finds out I'm in the military, it'll kill whatever chance I have of getting the information you want."

Leah frowned in concentration as she fussed with the strands of ivy draping the tiered crystal pedestal centered on the sample table setting she had arranged. Once satisfied with the design, she would photograph the table, note the style and color of linens used, as well as the other accessories, and record them all in the client's file to reference for the wedding reception scheduled for October.

"Looks good."

Leah glanced over at Kate, her assistant, then back at the centerpiece and worried her lip. "You don't think the ivy will obstruct the guests' views?"

"You're just obsessing because Mrs. Snotgrass is the client."

"*Snod*grass," Leah corrected. "If you're not careful, you're going to slip and call her that one day."

"It would be worth it just to see the expression on the old biddy's face."

"Easy for you to say. It isn't your business she'd send down the toilet."

Kate snorted. "As if she could."

Leah lifted the digital camera hanging from her neck and moved around the table, clicking off shots of the table from different angles. "Though I appreciate the vote of confidence, Mrs. Snodgrass's opinion carries a lot of weight in this town. One derogatory comment from her and my business would suffer the reverberations for months."

Satisfied that she'd taken enough pictures to record all the accessories used in the design, she headed for her office to download the photos into the appropriate file.

Kate trailed behind. "How's the search going for the mechanic?"

"I found one."

Kate dropped down into the chair opposite Leah's desk and lifted a brow. "Really? Who?"

"Sam Forrester."

"Never heard of him."

"He's not from around here."

"Then how's he going to do the work?"

"He's staying in the apartment over the garage."

Kate sat bolt upright. "A complete stranger? Have you lost your mind?"

"I checked his references," Leah said defensively.

Scowling, Kate slouched back in the chair. "Which doesn't mean squat. The references he gave could all be his friends."

Leah caught her lower lip between her teeth, having thought the same thing, then shook her head. "No. He seems like an honest guy. He even agreed to allow Craig to help with the restoration."

"He's probably cleaning out your house as we speak."

"Would you stop?" Leah cried. "You haven't even met the man."

Kate rose. "Then introduce me."

Leah looked up at her blankly. "Now?"

Kate shrugged. "No time like the present. We can grab some lunch on the way back."

"And who would mind the shop while we're gone?" Shaking her head, Leah plucked her purse from beneath her desk and headed out.

"Where are you going?" Kate asked, following her.

"I—I forgot something at home."

Kate bit back a smile. "Liar. You're going to check on the mechanic."

Leah opened her mouth to deny the statement, then clamped it shut and marched out the door, her chin in the air.

* * *

Settling into the apartment above Leah's garage took Sam all of about five seconds. All he had with him was crammed into his duffel bag, which consisted of about four changes of clothes, his toiletries and an extra pair of boots—all civilian wear, since he was on a monthlong leave from the army.

He'd just dumped his underwear and undershirts into a drawer when he heard a tap on the exterior door.

"Come on in," he called. "It's open."

Just as he stepped from the bedroom and into the sitting room, Leah was bumping the front door closed with her hip. And a nice curvy set of hips at that, he noted.

She lifted her arms, indicating a stack of towels and washcloths. "Thought you might need these. My cousin and her husband were my last guests, and I forgot to restock the linen closet after doing the laundry."

"Thanks." He took the linens from her and set them on the antique trunk that served as a coffee table. "And speaking of laundry…do you mind if I use your washer and dryer? I'll supply my own detergent."

"Help yourself. It's off the kitchen. The controls are self-explanatory, but let me know if you have any problems."

"I'm sure I can figure it out."

When she didn't make a move to leave, he looked at her curiously. "Was there something else?"

Avoiding his gaze, she picked up a pillow from the sofa. "About your references…" she began uncertainly as she plucked at its corded edge.

"Is there a problem?"

"No. No problem. In fact, they were all glowing." Huffing a breath, she tossed the pillow to the sofa and turned to face him. "Yes, there *is* a problem. Not a one of the men I spoke with mentioned anything about your past work history."

Though he knew he was treading on dangerous ground, Sam wasn't worried. He'd gotten himself out of tighter spots in the past. "Probably because I've never worked directly for any of them." He gestured to the sofa. "Have a seat," he invited. "I'll answer whatever questions you might have."

She hesitated a moment, then sat down at the far end of the sofa. "Just for a minute. I need to get back to the shop."

Dropping down on the opposite end, he draped his arm along the back of the sofa and opened his hand. "Fire away."

"You might start by explaining how you have a month available to devote to this project."

"That's simple enough. I'm taking what might be called a sabbatical while I consider a career change."

She looked at him curiously. "You don't like working as a mechanic?"

"Oh, I enjoy working on cars well enough," he replied, neatly avoiding a lie. "Always have. In fact, I think I was about fourteen when I rebuilt my first engine."

Her eyebrows shot up. "*Fourteen?* That's not even the legal age to drive a car!"

Chuckling, he shook his head. "No, but it's legal to work on one. My dad was a rancher, but his first love was cars. Especially vintage models. While most of the boys my age were playing with baseballs and bats, I was pulling engines and rebuilding carburetors." Before she could ask another question about his past, he shifted the conversation to her. "Did you have any weird hobbies when you were a kid?"

She blew out a breath. "I didn't rebuild cars, that's for sure. My only hobby—if you would call it that—was arranging flowers."

"Your mother was a florist?"

She snorted a breath. "Hardly. Our neighbor was. She ran a floral business out of her home. I hung out there while growing up."

Hoping to take advantage of this opening to learn more about her, as well as her family, he angled a leg onto the sofa and faced her. "She let you help her make floral arrangements?"

"Not at first. In the beginning I was more like a gofer. Fetching supplies, sweeping up the cuttings, that kind of thing. I eventually graduated to making my own designs, but that was years later."

"Do you remember your first?"

Her face softened at the memory. "A baby gift for a new mother. The vase was a ceramic baby carriage. I filled it with pink carnations, baby's breath and greenery." She shot him a sideways glance, her expression sheepish. "Not very original, huh?"

He shrugged. "Everybody has to start somewhere."

"Well, that was definitely my defining moment. I was hooked from then on and never looked back."

Although he knew about the business she currently owned, she wasn't aware he did. "So you're a florist?"

"In a sense. I own my own company. Stylized Events. We handle all the details of a party, from invitation to cleanup and everything in between, including floral arrangements, depending on a client's preferences."

He shuddered. "Sounds like a lot of work to me."

"It is," she agreed. "But I love it." She wrinkled her nose. "Or I do most of the time."

"Uh-oh. Contrary clients?"

She laughed softly. "Only one, really. Mrs. Snodgrass—or *Snot*grass, as my assistant refers to her."

He laughed. "Obviously your assistant believes in calling a spade a spade."

Grimacing, she grumbled, "Which is why I'm here."

He lifted a brow. "And why is that?"

She dropped her gaze, obviously embarrassed that she'd let that slip. "Kate thinks I was a little…well, hasty in allowing you to move into the apartment."

"A cautious woman," he commended with a nod of approval. "But in this case misguided." He slid his hand from the sofa and laid it on her shoulder, drawing her gaze to his. "I assure you you're safe with me."

"I doubt she'd consider that assurance comforting, coming from you."

Smiling, he drew his hand back to rest on the back of the sofa again. "Probably not, but in time I'll prove I'm trustworthy."

"Speaking of time…" She glanced at her wristwatch and rose. "I better get back to the shop. I've been away too long as it is."

He stood and followed her to the door. "I hope you don't mind, but I nosed around some in the garage this morning. Looks like you have all the tools I'll need to get started on the car."

She paused in the open doorway. "They were my brother's. When I had his car towed over here, I had them bring his tools, too."

With her back to him, he couldn't see her expression, but he was sure he caught a hint of sadness in her voice.

"The two of you…" he began hesitantly. "Were you close?"

She stood there a long moment, then heaved a sigh and started down the stairs. "Yeah, we were."

Two

Having lived in other areas of the world for the last several years, Sam had forgotten how hot Texas summers could get. In a matter of hours, the temperature in the garage rose from a slow simmer to a rolling boil, leaving him drenched in sweat and struggling for every breath.

After two days of sweltering in the garage, he decided a change of venue was necessary if he hoped to make any progress on the car. He scoped out possible locations, then raised the garage door and pushed the Mustang out onto the driveway. With the sun beating down on him like a blowtorch, he pushed and strained some more until he'd maneuvered the car beneath the shade of the breezeway.

Deciding that the new location was a bit more bearable, he fetched tools from the garage, then lay down on the creeper and pushed himself beneath the car to examine the underside.

After a careful inspection, he decided, considering its age, the undercarriage wasn't in too bad a shape. Not that it was going to be easy to repair the damage that thousands of miles and years of neglect had inflicted. He tapped a wrench against a brace and was rewarded with a shower of powdery rust. No, he thought, dragging a hand across his eyes to clear them, this wasn't going to be easy.

He used his boot heel to push the creeper along, following the line of the exhaust pipe to the rear of the car, and noted that rust corroded the entire system from the connection at the engine all the way to the rear bumper. Pulling a pencil stub and scrap of paper from his jeans pocket, he scribbled *muffler* and *tailpipe* on the growing list of parts he would need.

He was wheeling himself from beneath the car when he heard the scrape of footsteps on the drive. Hauling himself to his feet, he glanced in that direction and saw Craig heading up the drive.

Smiling a welcome, he pulled a rag from his back pocket to wipe his hands. "Hey, Craig! How's it going?"

Craig shrugged but didn't slow down. "All right, I guess."

Sam gestured toward the car. "You're just in time to help remove the exhaust pipe."

"Got homework," Craig mumbled and passed him by.

Sam watched him in silence, surprised by the kid's refusal, as he specifically remembered Leah telling him the kid wanted to help with the restoration.

Shaking his head, he hunkered down in front of the rolling tool cart and selected a couple of wrenches from one of the drawers, then stretched out on the creeper again and wheeled himself beneath the car.

He wasn't going to push, he told himself. If the kid wanted to help, he'd let him.

And if he didn't…well, Sam would figure out a way to rope him into getting involved.

Leah braked to a stop on the drive, her eyes widening in dismay at the mess that blocked the breezeway and her normal path to the garage. In the middle of the destruction sat the Mustang, its hood up and its doors propped wide, looking like a bird preparing for flight. Tools of every description were scattered over the drive and along the car's fenders. A muffler and a twisted tailpipe lay in the flower bed that ran along the side of the house, crushing the blooms of her geraniums.

Incensed, she leaped from her car and marched to the partially dismantled Mustang and the man whose head was hidden beneath the hood.

"What on earth do you think you're doing?" she demanded angrily.

Sam drew his head from beneath the hood only far enough to look at her. "Working on the car. What does it look like I'm doing?"

"Destroying my yard, that's what!" She flung out an arm. "Just look at this mess! You've turned my driveway into a junkyard!"

"What the hell did you expect?" he asked impatiently. "A car has to be dismantled before it can be restored."

Pulling a rag from his hip pocket, he straightened, dragging it down his face and chest. Her jaw dropped when she saw that he wasn't wearing a shirt. Glancing quickly around to see if any of the neighbors were watching, she grabbed him by the elbow and hustled him into the backyard. "You can't parade around half-dressed," she whispered angrily. "What will my neighbors think?"

He jerked his arm from her grasp. "I don't give a tinker's damn what your neighbors think. It's hot as hell out here. Wearing a shirt makes it that much hotter."

Flattening her lips, she folded her arms across her breasts. "I suppose I should be glad you didn't take off your pants."

He reached for the first button on his jeans. "Now that you mention it—"

She slapped his hand. "Don't you dare!"

In the blink of an eye she found her hand in his grasp and her body thrust up against his, his face inches from her own.

"I've never struck a woman in my life," he informed her coldly, "but slap at me again, and I might consider it."

She gulped. "I—I just wanted to stop you from taking off your jeans."

His scowl deepened. "Believe it or not, I have a few scruples, one of which is not bearing my ass in public. So there's no need for you to worry that pretty little head of yours that I'll strip naked and flash your snooty neighbors.

"And as far as the mess on your driveway goes," he continued, "it's too damn hot to work in the garage. I pushed the car out here, where I could get some air. But if having all this *junk,* as you call it, scattered around upsets your anal-retentive personality, you didn't have to jump me about it. All you had to do was ask and I'd have moved it to the back and out of sight."

He released her and took a step back. "Now," he said, and used the rag to wipe his hands, "is there anything else bothering you?"

She gulped again. Swallowed. "N-no."

"Good." He stuffed the rag back into his hip pocket. "So? How was your day?"

Thrown off balance by his quick mood change, it took her a moment to find her voice. "B-busy."

"Yeah, mine, too." He picked up the wrench he'd set aside and returned it to the tool cart. "You ought to do something about that tension in your shoulders. It's bad for your health."

She started to roll her shoulders, then squared them instead. "I had a stressful day."

"I take it Mrs. Snotgrass dropped by."

She blinked, surprised that he'd remembered her client's name. "*Snod*grass," she corrected. "And yes, she was in the shop this afternoon."

He rolled the tool cart closer to the car. "I noticed there's a spa attached to your pool. You ought to put it to use. Let it work out some of the kinks in your shoulders."

"I'll keep that in mind."

"If it's all right with you, I might use it later." He dropped a wrench into the drawer, then flexed his arm. "I used muscles today I haven't used in a while."

She stared in fascination at the play of sinew beneath his sweat-slickened skin. "F-fine with me."

"Appreciate it." He stooped and picked up a pair of pliers, tossed them into an open drawer. "Craig's home."

At the mention of her nephew, she glanced toward the house, then back at Sam and frowned. "Why isn't he helping you?"

"Said he had homework."

Her scowl deepened. "He pulls that card when he doesn't want to do something."

He glanced over his shoulder. "I thought you said he wanted to help with the car?"

"He does—did." She lifted her hands, then dropped them helplessly to her sides. "I don't know what he wants anymore. The last couple of weeks he's withdrawn more and more into himself, refuses to talk me. I was hoping that restoring the car would pull him out of whatever funk he's in. Breathe some life back into him."

"Where's his mother? Why doesn't she do something to help him?"

She shook her head sadly at the mention of her sister-in-law. "Patrice is buried so deep in her own grief half the time she's not even aware Craig's around."

He frowned thoughtfully as he wiped the grease from a wrench. "I could have a go at him if you want. See if I can get him back on track." He tossed the wrench into a drawer, bumped it shut with his knee. "He might respond to a man quicker than he would a woman."

She looked at him in puzzlement, surprised by his offer. "Why would you want to do that? You don't even know Craig. "

He shrugged. "Losing a dad can screw with a kid's head. Having a man to talk to, hang out with, might help him open up, share what's on his mind."

She opened a hand in invitation. "If you think you can help him, be my guest."

"You may not like my methods. If you don't, you have to promise not to interfere."

She'd done her own research on the subject of troubled teens and was familiar with some of the commonly used methods—tough love, wilderness survival training, behavior modification—and the names alone were enough to terrify her. "He won't be in any danger, will he?" she asked uneasily.

He gave her a droll look. "I wasn't planning on torturing the kid."

She didn't find his assurance all that comforting, considering his earlier rough treatment of her. But she feared if something wasn't done soon, she was going to lose Craig, either to drugs…or, worse, to suicide. Chilled by the thought, she drew in a steadying breath. "Just the same, I don't want him hurt."

He stripped off the pad he'd used to protect his stomach while working on the engine and turned away. "Too late. He's already hurt."

The sunroom at the rear of Leah's house was her favorite room in the house. Shortly after moving in, she'd painted the walls a soft buttery yellow and the ceiling with a mural of a cloud-filled sky. She'd chosen wicker to fill the space and positioned the chairs in front of the casement windows to capture the best views of her pool and landscaped backyard.

In the daytime sunlight flooded the room, creating a sunny and cheery nook in which to relax. At night it was no less restful, with lamplight washing the room with a soft golden glow.

But on this particular night the sunroom failed to work its magic charm for Leah.

Seated in a wicker chair, her feet propped on the matching ottoman, her thoughts were anything but restful as she stared at the apartment over the garage, considering the man inside.

She didn't know what to make of Sam Forrester. He both baffled and intrigued her. She didn't particularly care for the rough way he'd treated her earlier when she'd confronted him about the mess he'd made of her yard. But, in retrospect, she supposed she'd had it coming. She *had* slapped at him, as he'd accused her of doing.

Yet, in spite of now knowing that he could become physical when provoked, she wasn't afraid of him. That knowledge was simply something she'd keep in mind the next time she decided to go toe-to-toe with him.

But she was still a little miffed about the "anal-retentive" comment.

She wasn't obsessive, she told herself. She simply appreciated order. She supposed growing up in a home in which disorder reigned might have influenced her desire for neatness. But she certainly didn't consider that a personality fault. To her it was a virtue, a method of survival.

She frowned thoughtfully as she considered again his offer to serve as a mentor of sorts for her nephew. A man who was willing to befriend a troubled teenager couldn't be all bad, she told herself. But what she couldn't figure out was why he would want to do something like that. He didn't know Craig, had no ties to him. Why would he care one way or the other what happened to him?

As she continued to stare, the door to the apartment opened, and her thoughts shattered as Sam stepped out. She gaped when she saw that he was wearing swim trunks and carried a towel draped over his shoulder. Sliding farther down in her chair, she watched him cross to the spa. The lights in the backyard were off, but the lights in the pool and spa were on, offering enough illumination for her to see his movements...as well as his physique.

A slow shiver chased down her spine as she remembered being held against that body that afternoon. The damp heat that had seeped through her blouse, the muscled wall of chest crushed against her breasts. She shivered again at the memory as he tossed the towel onto a chair and sat down on the spa's stone edge. He dipped his fingers into the water, testing the temperature, then glanced toward the house.

She froze, realizing that with the lamp on she was clearly visible. A smile spread across his face as he spotted her, and he motioned for her to join him. She considered ignoring the invitation, planning to tell him, if questioned later, that she had dozed off in the chair and hadn't seen him.

He robbed her of that excuse by rising and striding toward the house. Prepared to send him on his way, she met him at the French door that opened to the outside.

He greeted her with a friendly smile. "Come on out and join me. The water's just right."

It was an effort, but she managed to keep her gaze fixed on his face and not let it slip to the magnificent view of his chest. "Thanks, but I was just about to head upstairs for the night."

"It's too early to go to bed," he chided. "Besides, you'll sleep better after relaxing in the spa for a while."

"No, really, I…"

He leveled a finger at her nose. "You have exactly five minutes to change into a swimsuit," he warned. "Then I'm coming after you."

Before she could refuse again, he turned and walked away. Frowning, she closed the door. She considered locking it but knew that would be a waste of time, since she'd given him a key to her house in order for him to have access to the kitchen and laundry room.

Surely he wouldn't make good his threat, she told herself.

"Four minutes, thirty seconds," he called loudly.

Convinced that he would, she ran for the stairs and raced up to change into her swimsuit.

Breathless and with only seconds to spare, she hurried outside to find Sam already sitting in the spa. Chest-deep in the bubbling water, his arms spread along the spa's stone edge, he watched her approach.

Feeling uncomfortably conspicuous, she unwrapped the towel she'd cinched at her waist and carefully folded it before placing it on the chair with his.

As she turned for the spa, she saw the amusement on his face and stopped. "What?"

He tipped his head toward the towel. "Are you sure you got all the wrinkles out? You might have missed one or two."

She jutted her chin, remembering his anal-retentive comment. "Just because I'm careful with my things doesn't make me anal."

"Uh-huh. Whatever you say." Water sluiced down his body as he rose and offered her a hand. "You're going to thank me for this later," he assured her as he helped her into the water.

"I wouldn't hold my breath," she muttered and snatched her hand from his. She sank onto the circular bench opposite him. Jets churned the warm water around her, making her skin tingle and the underwater lights dance beneath the surface.

With a contented sigh he dipped his head back and closed his eyes. "Heaven, huh?"

"It does feel good," she said, willing to concede only that much.

"Nothing eases sore muscles faster than a good soak in a spa. Other than a full-fledged massage," he amended, then lifted his head to peer at her through one eye. "I don't suppose you'd be willing to give me one?"

The smile she offered him was saccharine-sweet. "You're right. I wouldn't."

"I'd return the favor."

She shook her head, then couldn't help but laugh when he slid beneath the water, his face a mask of dejection.

Moments later he reemerged, slicking his hair back from his face.

She lifted a brow. "Kind of shallow for swimming, don't you think?"

He blinked the water from his eyes. "Wasn't trying to swim. I was checking out your legs."

She snatched her knees up and hugged them against her breasts. "If I'd known you'd invited me out here to ogle me, I would've stayed inside."

His smile smug, he reared back, splaying his arms along the spa's stone edge again. "Honey, me ogling you is the least of your worries."

She tried to frown but couldn't help but laugh. Pushing out a hand, she shot a spray of water at him. "You're incorrigible."

"No," he corrected, dragging a hand down his

face. "I'm just a man who recognizes a pretty woman when he sees one."

"Much more of your bull, and I'll need boots."

He shot her a wink. "No bull, ma'am. Just fact."

Deciding it best to ignore him, she slid farther down the wall of the tub and propped her feet against the bench opposite her, wanting to take advantage of the spa's therapeutic effects. The new position aimed jets of water at her upper back and shoulders, pulsing away at the tension knotted there. She would have purred her pleasure, but she refused to give Sam the opportunity to say I told you so.

"Tell me about your family," he said after a moment.

She opened her eyes wide enough to narrow them at him. "Why?"

"It might give me some insight into what's troubling Craig."

At the mention of her nephew she sat up, frowning thoughtfully as she swept her hair up to knot it on top of her head. "We don't have much family left. You already know about my father and brother. My mother died about five years ago, which just leaves Craig, Patrice and me."

"How did your mother die?"

"The official ruling was suicide, but I prefer to believe she grieved herself to death."

"Over the loss of your father?"

Uncomfortable with the subject, she plucked a

leaf from the bubbling water, trying to think how best to answer.

He lifted a brow at the action.

"That's not being anal," she informed him and dropped the leaf over the side of the tub. "It would end up in the filter anyway, which I have to clean out. I was just saving myself some time."

"Uh-huh."

Flattening her lips, she directed the conversation back to his question. "And yes, my mother never got over losing my father. She never gave up hope, either. She always believed he'd come home some day."

"Was Craig close to her?"

She shook her head. "No. Mom was so consumed with finding my dad she didn't have time for much else."

"She searched for him?"

"She didn't go to Vietnam, if that's what you mean. But she spent hours and hours combing through reports about POWs and MIAs, hoping to find some mention or reference of my dad." Knowing what most people thought of her mother's obsession, she grimaced. "You probably think she was crazy."

"Not in the least. A woman who loved her husband as deeply as your mother obviously did deserves my admiration, not my scorn."

Though surprised by his response, she didn't

pursue it, as she preferred not to talk about her parents. "Tell me about your family," she said instead.

"Not much to tell. I'm an only child. My parents divorced when I was fifteen. Dad moved to Atlanta, remarried and has three kids."

She gave him a chiding look. "And you said you didn't have siblings."

"Since I've never been allowed to see or talk to them, I don't consider them siblings."

"You've never even *seen* them?" she asked incredulously.

"Nope. My stepmother's rule. She likes to pretend I don't exist, that my dad's life began when he married her."

"And he puts up with that?"

"Not entirely. He and I get together a couple of times a year. At a neutral location," he added. "Never at their home."

Stunned, she sank back against the tile wall. "What a bitch."

"You won't get an argument out of me."

"What about your mother?" she asked after a moment. "Where is she?"

"In Seattle. Moved there after I graduated from high school. According to her, that was as far away from Dad as she could get without falling into the ocean."

She winced. "I take it their divorce was unpleasant."

"Their *marriage* was unpleasant."

"Fifteen," she said, thinking out loud. "That's a difficult age to have your parents divorce. It must have been hard on you."

"No worse than living with them while they were married."

She gave him a doubtful look. "Was it really that bad? I mean, I never lived with both my parents. Not that I remember, anyway. But I'd think there has to be something positive to be gained from having lived as a family, even if it was only for a short time."

He shook his head. "Can't prove it by me. My parents fought like cats and dogs. Rather than be caught in the crossfire, I stayed away from home as much as possible."

"But you said you and your father rebuilt cars together," she said in confusion. "Surely that would require you spending time together."

"We did. But only at his shop. That was the one place he could escape Mom."

She studied him curiously, intrigued by this part of his life he was sharing. "How did you react to their divorce?"

"Went a little wild. Was in trouble more often than not."

"What kind of trouble?"

"You name it, I did it at one time or another." He shook his head. "There was a guy I ran with. Ty

Bodean. He was rotten to the core, though I was too blind to see at the time. The two of us pretty much terrorized the town. It's a wonder somebody didn't kill us just to put us out of our misery."

As she listened, she found it easy to believe that he was once a bad boy. "You seem to have turned out all right."

"Thanks to Ty's half brother. He was always riding us about Ty's and my behavior and how we were going to screw up our lives if we didn't straighten up. Ty mostly tuned him out, but he never gave up on him. Or me, for that matter.

"The night we graduated from high school, Ty and I thought it would be fun to shoot the windows out of some of the stores downtown. Cops caught us and hauled us to jail. Ty called his half brother and he came and bailed us out. Ty thought he would just take us home, give us the standard lecture and that would be the end of it. Instead he drove us to the prison in McAllister and had the warden give us the grand tour. When we were done, he sat us both down and told us that he hoped we liked what we had seen because that was going to be our home if we didn't change our ways.

"Ty laughed off the warning, but I sure as hell didn't. Seeing the inside of that prison shook me clean to the bone. I guess his half brother realized there was hope for me yet, because he started spending time with me, talking to me about things.

More by his example than anything else, I began to see what a lowlife I had become and decided to clean up my act." He opened his hands. "So here I am, a reformed rake."

She released a long breath, having been caught up by his story. "Wow. You're lucky he cared enough to take you under his wing."

"Nobody knows that better than me. Fact is, I owe him my life."

She looked at him curiously. "That's why you offered to help Craig, isn't it? Because of what your friend's half-brother did for you?"

He shrugged. "Partly." Smiling, he scooted around on the bench and draped an arm along the edge of the tub behind her. "But mostly I did it because the kid's got a good-looking aunt."

With him so close, she could see nothing but his face. The chiseled line of cheekbone, smoky blue eyes, the sensual curve of his lips. Sure that he was about to kiss her, she nervously wet her lips. "I thought you said you were a *reformed* rake."

His lips curved higher, revealing the most adorable dimples.

"Even a reformed rake slips now and again." Cupping a hand at her cheek, he touched his lips to hers, withdrew with a low hum of pleasure, then returned for a second taste.

"Sweet," he murmured, tracing his tongue along her lower lip. Angling his body more fully toward hers, he pushed his fingers through her hair and took the kiss deeper, holding her face to his.

God help me, she thought weakly. Though every nerve in her body demanded she respond, intellectually she knew what a mistake that would be. Sam worked for her, and any kind of intimacy, no matter how innocent, could jeopardize their business relationship.

If that wasn't reason enough for her to put an end to this foolishness, he was a virtual stranger. She didn't know him. Not in the sense a woman needed to know a man before making out in a hot tub with him. More importantly, she didn't trust men. After the hell Louis had put her through, she had learned to keep her guard up when dealing with the male species.

In spite of all the reasons pointing her away from Sam, she found herself melting against him until every thought leaked from her mind save one. Him. The pleasure evoked by his lips. The strength in the hands that held her to him. The knee wedged firmly against her thigh. The tickle of stubble that rasped her chin and upper lip.

Much too soon, he dragged his mouth from hers. Disappointed that he'd ended the kiss, she forced open her eyes and found his gaze on her.

He stroked a thumb along her cheekbone, his smile slow, sexy. "Even better than I'd imagined."

It took her a moment to find her voice. "W-what?"

"Kissing you." He slid his hands down her back and looped them low at her waist. "And, believe me, what I'd imagined was already topping the charts."

Both pleased and embarrassed, she dropped her gaze, unsure what to say.

He saved her a reply by rising and taking her hand. "We better head in."

He climbed from the spa, then turned and helped her out. Plucking her towel from the chair, he draped it over her shoulders, then used its ends as a rope and tugged her to him for one last kiss.

Drawing back he smiled down at her. "Good night, Leah."

Finding it difficult to tear her gaze from his, she murmured, "'Night, Sam," then spun and hurried for the house before she did something really stupid.

Like drag him upstairs and chain him to her bed.

Three

Sam had known a lot of women in his life, but not a one of them had ever dominated his thoughts the way Leah did. He seldom thought of her without sex slipping into his mind, too. Legs that seemed to stretch forever. A firm, taut body. Lips ripe for kissing. Breasts begging to be touched.

"Thinking with your Johnson," he muttered under his breath as he strained to remove the frozen spark plugs from the Mustang's engine. And when a man let his Johnson do his thinking, he was asking for trouble. What he needed to do was focus on his real reason for being here: getting the information for Mack. He'd been a guest in her apartment for over a week and wasn't one whit closer to finding out what he needed to know.

The spark plug gave and the loss of pressure had him pitching forward. Heaving a weary sigh, he ducked from beneath the hood and dragged an arm across the sweat that dripped into his eyes. He cut a wistful glance at the pool, thinking a swim would feel really good about now. His gaze slid to the spa, and an image of Leah rose in his mind, her damp hair twisted up on top of her head, her breasts pushing at the scrap of fabric that covered them. With a groan, he dropped the wrench and headed for the house, hoping a cold drink of water would cool his thoughts.

At the back door he toed off his boots, knowing Leah would pitch a walleyed fit if he tracked grease onto her pristine floors. Once inside, he poured himself a glass of cold water from the container in the fridge, tipped the glass back and emptied it in three long gulps.

His thirst quenched for the moment, he back-handed the moisture from his mouth, propped his hips against the edge of the cabinet and looked around. As usual, the kitchen was neat as a pin, with not so much as a dish towel out of place.

It was also eerily quiet, as was the rest of the house. Not surprising, since Leah was at work and Craig at school.

Slowly becoming aware of a loud, rhythmic

ticking sound in the silence, curious, he walked through the house, tracing it to the entry hall, where a stately grandfather clock stood like a sentry against one wall. Obviously an antique, the heavily carved piece consisted of two sections, the upper-most framing the face of the clock. In the glass-encased lower portion a brass pendulum slowly swung from side to side.

Satisfied that he'd identified the ticking sound and that the house wasn't about to blow up, he headed back to the kitchen. As he passed through the den, he slowed, his gaze drawn to the wall of bookshelves on his right. Wondering what kind of literature appealed to a woman like Leah, he moved to stand before the unit and scanned the books' spines. Gardening, psychology, interior design, biographies and a couple of paperback mystery novels. Amused by the wide range of subject matter, he started to turn away but stopped when he spotted a photo album lying on the bottom shelf.

Judging by its worn cover, he assumed it was from her youth, possibly even dating before her birth. He was tempted to pick it up and look through it, hoping to find information about her dad—spe-cifically the piece of paper Mack had requested he locate. But snooping through her things would violate the trust Leah had placed in him when she'd given him the key to her house.

He vacillated a moment while his conscience and his curiosity duked it out.

With a resigned sigh, he turned his back on the tempting album and headed for the kitchen, his conscience, as well as his integrity, still intact.

Just as he stepped outside to resume his work on the Mustang, Leah's SUV turned onto the drive. Relieved that he hadn't given in to the temptation to snoop, he watched her leap from the vehicle and run for the house. When she dashed past him, without so much as a how-do-you-do, he grabbed her arm. "Hey. Where's the fire?"

She tugged free. "Haven't got time to explain," she said breathlessly as she yanked open the kitchen door. "I'm in panic mode."

Panic mode? Shaking his head, he watched her disappear inside the house, thinking the woman lived in that state.

But she had seemed a little more stressed than usual, he thought with a frown. Could something have happened? Maybe to Craig?

Determined to find out what was up, he reached for the door and was nearly bowled over when she came flying back out.

"Wait a minute," he said as she rushed past him. "What's going on?"

She called over her shoulder, "Later. Gotta go."

Sure that concern for her nephew was the only thing that would cause her this level of distress, he plucked his T-shirt from the roof of the Mustang and ran after her, sliding into the passenger seat just as she pulled the gearshift into reverse.

"What do you think you're doing?" she cried. "I need to go!"

"Then go. I'm not stopping you."

She set her jaw. "I have exactly four hours to set up for a party. Would you please just get out? I'm already late."

"Don't get all huffy with me. If you're late, it's your fault, not mine."

"It isn't my fault! I only got the call ten minutes ago! Now will you *please* get out?"

"Not until you tell me what's going on."

She pressed a hand to her forehead and inhaled a deep breath as if struggling for patience. "The job's for the city. I bid on it months ago, but the contract was awarded to another company. They bailed at the last minute, and now the city has asked me to step in." She looked at him with pleading eyes. "This is important. Really important. If I do a good job, it'll mean more business for me in the future. So, please, get out so I can go."

He clicked his seat belt into place. "You probably could use some help."

She clamped down on her jaw. "Fine," she said, grinding out the words, and reversed into the street. "But if you get bored, don't even think about asking me to bring you home, because I won't."

She stomped on the brake to shift into drive.

He braced a hand against the dash to keep from being thrown forward. "Oh, I doubt I'll get bored," he replied mildly. "Not with you behind the wheel."

With nothing left for him to do, Sam moved to the far end of the country club's ballroom and waited while Leah double-checked each table one last time. He shook his head as he watched her turn a centerpiece a millimeter to the left. The woman got way too caught up in details.

He still couldn't believe the warehouse she'd taken him to collect the equipment and supplies she'd needed. On the outside the building had looked like most of the others in the complex. It was the interior where the differences lay.

Row after row of shelving filled the cavernous space, each loaded with neatly stacked boxes and crates. Hanging from a clipboard at the beginning of each row, a laminated inventory listed all the items found on that row—in alphabetical order, no less. If that wasn't enough to prove her anal tendencies, a card was attached to each container, with a detailed description of its contents.

In spite of her obsessiveness for organization, he had to admit the woman knew what she was doing when it came to decorating for an event. To satisfy her client's request for a patriotic theme, she had designed centerpieces using white hydrangeas, blue delphiniums and red geraniums. She had come up with a pretty clever way of incorporating fireworks into the scheme, as well, by filling thin silver tubes with sprays of red, white and blue star garlands cut into varying lengths and placing them strategically among the flowers in the centerpiece. When the votive candles scattered around the tables were lit, the multicolored foil stars shimmered and sparkled like fireworks exploding on the Fourth of July.

Sam had helped create the faux fireworks, but he'd spent the majority of his time setting up tables and chairs and draping the tables with—get this—*three* tablecloths, arranged by size, starting with the largest and ending with the smallest, which Leah had informed him was called a topper. She'd had specific instructions for placing the cloths, and if he failed to spread one exactly as instructed, she'd stop whatever she was doing, march over and adjust the cloth herself.

He'd finally managed to escape her evil eye when Kate, her assistant, had asked him to help her put the fireworks together. Cute girl, he reflected, and *very* protective of her boss. When Leah had first introduced them, Kate had been polite enough. But during the early part of the afternoon he had caught her watching him suspiciously on several occasions. He supposed working with her on the fireworks had dispelled whatever doubts she had about him, because by the time she left she was laughing and joking with him as if they were old friends.

Reminded that only he and Leah remained, he glanced at his watch and decided it was time to put an end to her *anal*-yzing.

Crossing the room, he caught her elbow and gave it a tug. "Come on. I'll buy you dinner."

She tugged right back. "Not yet. I still have six more tables to check."

"They're fine," he assured her and all but dragged her from the room.

Though he succeeded in getting her to her SUV, he could tell her mind was still inside the ballroom and the decorations she'd set up. This became even more evident when she didn't kick up a fuss when he bundled her into the passenger seat and took the wheel himself.

"You don't think the centerpieces are too busy?" she asked uncertainly as he started the engine.

"No. They're fine."

She reached for the door handle. "Maybe I should remove the sparklers. Simple is sometimes best."

He grabbed her arm before she could climb out. "The sparklers or fireworks or whatever the heck you call them are sensational. In the morning you'll have guests lined up at your door wanting you to plan their next party."

His assurance was almost a direct quote from a comment Kate had made to him earlier, but since he shared her opinion, he didn't feel badly about offering it to Leah now.

She looked at him hopefully. "You really think so?"

"Wouldn't have said it if I didn't." He put the vehicle in gear before she could attempt to hop out again. "Do you stress about all the events you plan as much as you have over this one?"

"No—yes." She heaved a sigh. "I give my best to all my clients, but this job is really important."

He turned onto the main road, leaving the country club behind. "What's so special about this one? I'd think, if anything, you wouldn't care as much, since the bid was originally given to someone else."

"It should've been mine from the beginning."

He cut a glance her way at the bitterness he detected in her tone. "Why wasn't it?"

"My ex serves on the city council."

Louis Banks. He remembered reading about her ex-husband's business and civic activities during the search he'd done on the Internet.

"One man has that much power?" he asked doubtfully.

"The family does. The Banks family is what's known as 'old Tyler.' They've lived here for generations and, as a result, have clout out the wazoo. Four years ago I controlled eighty percent of the event-planning business in this area. Within a month of our divorce my business dropped twenty-five percent. By the end of the year it hit forty."

He stole a glance at her. "Is it still going down?"

"No." She quickly rapped her knuckles against

the dash. "Knock on wood. I've clawed and scraped my way back up. I haven't reached my former numbers, but I'm getting there. That's why this job is so important. It's my chance to get my foot back in the door with the city."

He scowled at the road ahead. "Screw 'em."

She turned her head to peer at him. "Excuse me?"

He tossed up a hand. "If they'd let a guy with his jockstrap in a twist influence their decisions, you don't need their business."

Sputtering a laugh, she turned to face the front again. "Don't I wish."

He spotted a restaurant ahead and slowed, thinking food would get her mind off the party, as well as her ex. "How about Italian?"

Wrinkling her nose, she shook her head. "I'm really not in the mood to deal with a crowd. How about I make something for us at home?"

He sped up. "I have a better idea. Let's order pizza in."

Sam topped off the wine in Leah's glass, then glanced at her empty plate. "Another slice of pizza?"

She sank back in her chair, holding her hands over her stomach. "No. I'm stuffed."

He set the wine bottle down, plucked a slice from the box and sank his teeth into the cheesy wedge as he settled back. Feeling her gaze, he glanced her way and found her smiling at him.

"Thanks."

He licked sauce from the corner of his mouth. "I should be the one thanking you for turning me on to Mario's. They throw a mean pizza."

She laughed softly. "I didn't mean buying my dinner, although I do appreciate it. You were a tremendous help today. I don't know what Kate and I would have done without you."

"You'd have managed." He picked up his wineglass to wash down the pizza. "Do you and Kate usually set up everything yourself? Handling those tables was no easy job."

"I usually hire temps to take care of whatever heavy lifting is necessary. Unfortunately, due to the short notice we received, no one was available."

"Then I'm glad I insisted on going along." Smiling, he tapped his glass to hers. "Here's to a successful event."

"Amen to that." She took a sip of her wine, then tipped her head back with a sigh and closed her eyes.

"Tired?" he asked.

She opened her eyes to smile at him. "Exhausted. But way too wired to sleep."

"Same here." He glanced around, then gestured at the lounge chairs beside the pool. "Why don't we sit out there, where we can be more comfortable?"

She scraped back her chair. "Good idea."

He let her take the lead, then followed. On

impulse, instead of sitting next to her, he moved to stand behind her chair and dropped his hands over her shoulders.

She struggled to sit up. "What are you doing?"

He drew her back against the chair. "Relax," he soothed as he pressed his thumbs into her tensed muscles. "I'm going to give you a massage."

Her shoulders remained rigid beneath his hands—whether from wariness or stress, he wasn't sure. But after a few minutes the tendons began to soften beneath his fingers' urging.

He leaned to peer over her head and saw that her face was lax, her eyes closed. Biting back a smile, he pushed his thumbs up the gentle curve of her neck, then down, letting them slide beneath the neckline of her shirt. Keeping one hand cupped on her shoulder, he pushed the thumb of the other along her shoulder blade, lengthening the muscle. Though innocent, the action dragged her shirt and bra strap to the edge of her shoulder.

The exposed skin was satin-smooth and tinted a soft golden-brown. Noticing that there wasn't a tan line, he wondered if she sunbathed topless. Curious, he continued the massage, easing her shirt and bra strap farther down her arm to reveal more of her chest, planning to search for a tan line.

He heard her low moan, felt a tightening of response in his groin, but managed to keep his fingers moving, continuing the massage, while he peeked over her head to see if he'd mistaken the sound.

Oh, man, he thought, stifling a groan as his gaze settled on the soft swell of her breasts and the shadowed valley between. And no tan line, which meant either she was blessed with olive skin tones or she sunbathed topless.

Deciding that her level of arousal was a hell of a lot more important than determining genes versus sun-kissed skin, he brought his hands back to her neck, then smoothed them down her front. She moaned again, and this time there was no mistaking the sound for anything but arousal.

Leaning over, he covered her mouth with his and captured the sound. Though he'd expected her to come up, kicking and clawing, her lips remained soft beneath his, pliant, accepting.

With him all but standing on his head, blood rushed to his head, pulsed in his ears. Knowing he couldn't maintain this position for long, he eased around to her side while managing to keep his mouth on hers. Since she still didn't offer an objection, he opened the top two buttons of her shirt. He felt the rush of her breath against his lips, the tremble that shook her…but detected nothing that indicated refusal or indignation. Taking her silence as assent, he cupped his hands over her breasts and drew back to meet her gaze. "Feeling more relaxed now?"

Eyes wide, she gulped. "Th-that was smooth, Forrester."

"Think so?" Grinning, he gave her breasts a playful squeeze, then caught her hand, pulled her up. "Let's go skinny-dipping." He grabbed the bottom of his T-shirt, ripped it over his head and reached for the snap of his jeans.

She lunged forward and clamped her hand over his. "I'm not going skinny-dipping with you."

"Why not?"

"Because—because public nudity is against the law."

Hiding a smile, he dropped his gaze to her chest and dragged a finger along her shoulder. "No tan lines," he said, then lifted his gaze to hers in challenge. "You must not be too particular about breaking the law." With a shrug, he hooked his thumbs in the waist of his jeans. "But if it'll make you feel better, we'll leave our underwear on."

Not giving her time to argue, he stripped off his jeans, kicked them aside, then crossed to the edge of the pool and dipped a foot into the water. "The temperature is just right," he called to her.

Without waiting to see if she'd follow his lead, he sprang to his toes and dived in.

Leah stared at the ever-widening ring that marked the spot where Sam had disappeared into the pool. She shouldn't do this, she told herself. She should go inside and leave him to skinny-dip alone, if that's what he wanted to do. Just because he'd turned her into a puddle of quivering need with his dang seductive massage didn't mean she had to lose her senses completely.

But, oh, God, how she wanted to, she thought, gulping. It had been so long since she'd done anything wild, so totally uninhibited. And it seemed like forever since she'd felt anything close to desire.

As she continued to waver uncertainly, he surfaced on the far side of the pool, scraping his hair back from his face. Treading water, he called to her, "What are you waiting for? Come on in. The water's great."

She shouldn't, she told herself. This was insane, crazy. He was a flirt, a sex maniac.

Oh, God, she thought again and rose, stripping off her blouse and shoving down her shorts. Bare but for her flesh-colored bra and panties, she moved to the edge of the pool, drew in a steadying breath, then dived in.

Seconds later she burst from the water, her mouth open and gasping. "You liar!" she cried. "This water is freezing!"

He swam a few strokes to meet her. "Probably seems that way since you were so hot when you got in."

She flattened her lips, wanting to hang on to her anger with him, then sputtered a laugh. "You are hopeless."

"Incorrigible, hopeless," he said, reciting the adjectives she'd used to describe him. "It's a wonder my head doesn't swell with all the compliments you shower me with."

Rolling her eyes, she struck off for the shallower end of the pool. Sam followed, matching her stroke for stroke. When they reached the end, she climbed from the water and flopped down on the highest step, while he hauled himself up to sit beside her.

Gathering her hair between her hands, she twisted it into a long rope and squeezed, noticing that Sam watched the water drip onto her chest. Seemingly fascinated, he reached to trail his finger along the path of one droplet as it trickled down. When his finger dipped between her breasts, she sucked in a shocked breath.

He lifted his eyes to hers, and she gulped at the heat that darkened his blue eyes.

Hooking a finger in the front closure of her bra, he hauled her to him.

"Enough foreplay," he murmured and nipped at her lips. "It's time we got down to business."

"Sam…" she began weakly.

He dipped his head to nuzzle her neck and cupped her breast. "That's my name."

"I don't think—" He squeezed, kneading her flesh, and she dropped her head back with a groan. "Oh, Sam."

Hiding a smile, he kissed his way up her neck to

her mouth. "I like the way you turn my name into two syllables instead of just the one." He rolled her nipple between two fingers. "Really turns me on."

"And *that,*" she said with a shiver, "turns me on."

"Then let's kick up the speed a bit." He flicked open the front closure of her bra, freeing her breasts, then used his mouth to force her back against the edge of the pool.

She gasped at the contact, then knotted her fingers in his hair and clung as he suckled greedily. She didn't even consider asking him to stop. She needed this, him. Deserved it after four long years of celibacy.

He shifted, drawing her body to position between his thighs, then focused his attention on her breasts again.

In the distance, music played softly from the outdoor speakers hidden beneath the eaves of the house. A blues number, the whine of the sax sexy and low. The only other sound in the night came from the water's rhythmic lapping against the sides of the pool. Combined, they provided the perfect accompaniment for a slow seduction.

But Leah wasn't sure she could endure slow. It had been too long since she'd been with a man, and this one was unbelievably skilled with his mouth, his hands.

Anxious to touch him, too, she closed her fingers around his sex and was stunned to find him already rock-hard beneath his boxers. She stroked her fingers down his length, up, but soon became frustrated by the fabric that kept her from touching him fully and slipped her fingers inside the fly.

He flinched at the contact, then groaned and dropped his forehead to hers. "Leah?"

She gulped, barely able to breathe. "What?"

"Are you on the pill?"

Thrown off by the question, she drew back slowly to peer at him. "Well…no."

His shoulders sagged. "Damn. I was afraid you were going to say that." Heaving a sigh, he flopped down on the step next to her and dropped his head to his hands. "And to think I was once a Boy Scout," he said miserably.

She sat up slowly, drawing the cups of her bra together and fastening them into place while trying to reconcile her mind, as well as her throbbing body, that her celibacy wasn't going to end that night. "What does being a Boy Scout have to do with anything?"

"'Be prepared.' It's the motto Boy Scouts live by."

She rolled her lips inward, trying her best not to laugh.

He glanced her way and bumped his shoulder against hers. "Cut it out. This isn't funny."

"No," she agreed, then doubled over, laughing. "It's hysterical!"

* * *

Leah entered the last figure into her calculator, then hit the total button. After typing the amount into the appropriate column on the spreadsheet, she hit save, then sank back in her chair with a sigh of relief, the dreaded paperwork done for the day.

She should've finished earlier—and would have if she'd been able to keep her mind on her work and off Sam. She chuckled, remembering his disappointed expression when he'd admitted to his failure to live up to the Boy Scouts motto of Be Prepared. He could be so darn cute at times. At others, totally irresistible.

He had his faults, she reminded herself and straightened to tuck the invoices she'd recorded back into the file. He was stubborn, cocky and more than a little overbearing.

He was also kind and thoughtful and unbelievably sexy.

Kate stuck her head into her office. "Last customer just left."

Leah shot to her feet. "Quick. Put the Closed sign in the window before anyone else can get inside."

Tapping a finger to her temple in a salute, Kate disappeared from sight.

Leah quickly shut down her computer, snagged her purse from beneath her desk, then headed out, slowing only long enough to switch off her office light.

"How about a glass of wine?" Kate suggested. "My treat."

Leah hesitated a moment. She knew it was ridiculous, but she wanted to go home and see Sam.

But then she remembered that this was Kate's husband Frank's, night to play softball with the guys, which meant Kate would be alone. "Sounds good," she said, forcing a smile. "But I'm buying. You deserve a reward for the extra hours you put in this week."

"Won't get an argument out of me," Kate replied and led the way to the front door. "Let's try out that new bar on the corner. I hear they serve nachos during happy hour. I'm starving."

"Fine with me." Leah locked the door, then walked with Kate the short half block to the bar. Once inside, she hesitated, daunted by the number of people already crowded into the room. She glanced back toward the doorway. "Maybe we should try someplace else," she suggested hopefully.

Kate looped her arm through Leah's. "No way," she said as she dragged her into the melee. "I skipped lunch, remember? Another second without sustenance and I'll faint dead away." Spotting a couple leaving, Kate tugged Leah in that direction and pushed her into the booth they'd occupied before someone else could claim it.

"Chardonnay okay with you?" she asked.

Leah flapped a hand as she pulled a credit card from her purse to give to Kate. "Whatever you're drinking is fine with me. Tell the bartender to open a tab." While Kate went to the bar to order their drinks, Leah pulled out her cell phone and punched in her home number, wanting to let Craig know that she would be late. After four rings, the answering machine clicked on. Frowning, she disconnected the call.

Kate returned, setting a glass of wine in front of Leah. "Problem?"

Leah slid the phone back into her purse. "I called the house, but Craig didn't answer."

Shrugging, Kate took a sip of her drink. "Maybe Patrice picked him up early for a change."

Leah gave her a pointed look.

"Okay," Kate conceded reluctantly. "So the woman isn't a contender for Mother of the Year."

"That's putting it mildly," Leah said drily, then winced. "Maybe I should go home and check on him. Just to be safe."

Kate narrowed an eye. "You're not going anywhere. Craig is old enough to look after himself. Besides, Sam's there, isn't he?"

"Probably."

"So if the house caught fire or something equally bad had happened, Sam would call you, right?"

"I suppose."

"Then there's no reason for you to worry." Kate lifted her glass in a toast and smiled. "Here's to another successful event staged by the highly acclaimed Stylized Events."

Reminded of the complimentary mention her business had received in the morning newspaper, Leah tapped her glass against Kate's and added, "Which wouldn't have been possible without the help of my talented assistant."

Kate took a sip of her wine. "Not that I don't adore praise, but Sam deserves a chunk of the credit. I swear, that man's got muscles on top of muscles. Did you see the way he was tossing those tables around? As if they were made of paper instead of two tons of metal and wood."

"He was definitely a lifesaver," Leah agreed.

"And he even helped make the sparklers. Frank would cut off his right arm before he'd touch anything crafty like that. 'Girl stuff,' he calls it." She huffed. "He acts like any activity that doesn't end in the word *ball* will emasculate him."

Leah chuckled, always entertained by Kate's exaggerated stories about her husband Frank. "I have to admit, Sam surprised me with his willingness to tackle whatever we put in front of him."

"And he's such a hottie, too. Have you checked out his butt? The man's got a body to die for."

Leah took a sip of her wine to avoid Kate's gaze. "He's okay, I guess."

Kate choked a breath. "Are you blind? He's drop-dead gorgeous!"

When Leah said nothing, Kate narrowed her eyes. "Oh, I get it," she said slowly. "You've got the hots for him and don't want to admit it."

Leah dropped her mouth open, then quickly looked around to make sure no one had overheard. "I do not," she whispered angrily. "And would you please lower your voice. I'd prefer my personal life remain private."

Kate hooted a laugh. "So there is something going on between you two." She braced her arms on the table and leaned forward expectantly. "Spill. I want all the details."

Leah drew back and took a nervous sip of her wine. "There's nothing to tell."

As stubborn as a bulldog once she sank her teeth into something, Kate leaned closer. "I bet he's a good kisser, isn't he?"

Leah felt a blush creep up her neck. "If you like your job, you'll drop this subject, and I mean *now*."

"Come on, Leah," she begged. "Give an old married a woman a thrill."

"Three years of marriage doesn't qualify as 'old.'"

"It does when you're married to ESPN. Come on, share. Wet? Dry? French?"

Leah rolled her eyes. "You're sick. Really sick."

"I'll bet he Frenches."

Leah dropped her forehead to the table with a moan.

"Uh-oh," Kate murmured. "Trouble at six o'clock."

Leah jerked up her head, knowing by Kate's tone what she meant by *trouble*.

"Well, look who's here," a male voice said from behind her.

Leah set her jaw, then turned to greet her ex. "Why, Louis," she said, her smile as fake as his. "What a surprise seeing you here. Cheryl must have lengthened your leash. I don't believe I've ever seen you stray this far without her."

His eyes darkened at the sugarcoated barb, but he managed to keep his smile in place. "As a matter of fact, she'll be joining me soon."

Since she'd rather choke to death than breathe the same air as her ex and the woman he'd had an affair with through most of their married life, she glanced at her wristwatch.

"Would you look at the time?" she said in dismay and gathered her purse. "Sorry to rush off," she said as she rose and brushed past Louis, "but I need to get home and check on Craig."

"Please tell me you're not still playing nursemaid to that dysfunctional family of yours?"

The cruel remark struck her back like a knife, dragging her to a stop. Hauling in a deep breath, she forced herself on, telling herself it didn't matter. Louis's opinion was no longer important to her. She wasn't married to him any longer. And she certainly wasn't in love with him.

Sometimes she wondered if she ever was.

Four

That night, Leah lay in her bed, unable to sleep. Craig hadn't been home when she'd arrived, which alone would have been enough to keep her awake worrying about his safety, his whereabouts. The fact that Sam wasn't home, either, only increased her concerns.

She'd finally broken down and called her sister-in-law and was relieved when she'd overheard Craig talking to someone in the background. She had wanted to question Patrice about Craig's activities that afternoon, but she'd feared she would only upset her sister-in-law if she did. The woman was already teetering on the edge of emotional instability, and Leah wasn't about to take a chance on knocking her over the edge into a complete breakdown.

Knowing that Craig was safe should have relieved her enough to allow her to sleep. But her mind refused to shut down, building every possible scenario to explain Craig's break from their agreed routine.

Hoping a glass of warm milk would settle her nerves, she climbed from bed and tugged on her robe as she traipsed down the stairs. She had just pulled the milk from the refrigerator when she heard a noise behind her. Sure that it had come from the laundry room, she set the milk down and tiptoed toward the closed door. Easing it open, she peeked inside.

And found Sam sitting on the floor, his back propped against the dryer, reading a magazine.

She pushed the door wider. "What on earth are you doing?"

He looked up from the magazine, then laid it aside, his expression sheepish. "Sorry. I was trying to be quiet."

Distracted by his bare chest and the faded sweatpants that rode low on his hips, it took a moment for what he'd said to register. She shook her head. "You didn't wake me. I came downstairs to get a glass of milk."

"Trouble sleeping?"

She dragged a hand over her hair, assuming her wild hairstyle was what had given her away. Reluctant to share her concerns, especially after Louis's catty remark about her dysfunctional family, she said hesitantly, "Sort of," then decided she had to know. "Did you see Craig this afternoon?"

"Yeah. Not for long, though. He didn't get here until just before his mom came to pick him up. Why? Is there a problem?"

She paced the width of the laundry room and back, worrying her thumbnail. "I don't know. Kate invited me to have a glass of wine after work. I tried to call from the bar to tell Craig that I was going to be late, but I got the answering machine."

"He didn't get the message. I can vouch for him on that one, because he never went inside. Barely made it up the drive, before his mom showed up."

"Did he say where he'd been?"

He shook his head. "No. But, to be honest, we didn't talk. Wasn't time."

She wrung her hands. "I knew I shouldn't have gone with Kate. I should've come straight home like I always do."

He caught her hand and pulled her down to sit on the floor with him in front of the dryer. "Now don't go beating yourself up over this," he scolded gently. "You're entitled to a life, too."

She hugged her knees to her chest. "But he's my responsibility. If something had happened to him or he'd gotten into some kind of trouble, I'd never forgive myself."

"And you being home is going to prevent either of those things from happening?"

"Yes," she said defiantly.

"Come on, Leah. Even if you had been home, you couldn't have done anything. He wasn't *here* for you to protect."

She dropped her chin to her knees in dejection, knowing what he said was probably true.

He draped an arm around her shoulders and hauled her back to hug against his side. "Raising kids is hell, isn't it?

"You have no idea," she said miserably. She hesitated a moment, then decided he might as well know it all. "Craig's been running around with a different crowd lately. Some real losers, if you ask me. I haven't actually caught him at it, but I'm afraid he might be experimenting with drugs."

"Peer pressure is tough these days. A lot worse than when we were kids." He stretched out his legs and settled her more comfortably at his side. "But I wouldn't give up on Craig just yet. He seems like a good kid."

"He is…or was."

"Focus on *is,*" he ordered firmly, then gave her an encouraging smile. "He'll come around. You'll see. Heck, look at me. I got into more trouble than ten kids put together and I turned out all right."

In spite of her concern for her nephew, she bit back a smile. "In your opinion, maybe."

He drew back, feigning hurt. "You don't think I'm a nice guy?"

She lifted a shoulder. "You're okay, I guess."

"Just okay?" He heaved an exaggerated sigh. "Man, you really know how to hurt a guy."

She bumped her shoulder against his chest. "As if I could hurt that overinflated ego of yours."

Chuckling, he hugged her to his side. "So tell me did you and Kate have a good time?"

She shrugged again. "At first."

"Don't tell me you girls had a tiff?"

"No. Nothing like that. Louis showed up. My ex." Her anger returned as she remembered his parting remark. "He really knows what buttons to push to set me off. I can't believe I ever thought myself in love with him. He's heartless, cruel and would lie when the truth would serve him better."

"Sounds like a real charming fellow."

"Oh, he can be charming, all right," she said drily. "Don't doubt that for a minute. The problem is, it's usually when he wants something or after he's done something wrong and he's trying to weasel his way back into your good graces." She pressed her fingers to her temples and shook her head. "I don't want to talk about him. When I so much as *think* his name, I wind up with a headache."

"All right by me," he said agreeably. He waited a beat, then said, "I went shopping today."

She swept at a piece of lint that clung to her robe.

"I wondered where you were when I got home. What did you buy? More car parts?"

"That, too."

She glanced his way, wondering why he was being so evasive. "Am I supposed to guess?"

"That might be fun."

Hiding a smile, she gave him a slow look up and down. "Well, it certainly wasn't clothes."

"I'll give you a hint. Drugstore."

She stared, her smile fading as she realized what he'd bought. "Oh," she said, unable to think of a response.

He beamed a proud smile. "Giant economy-size package. Nearly gave the little white-haired lady at the checkout a heart attack."

She laughed, imagining him plopping his purchase down on the counter in front of some sweet old lady. "You probably did."

When he said nothing more, only looked at her expectantly, she lowered her gaze and plucked at the ends of her robe's sash. "This is awkward."

"Second thoughts?"

She shook her head. "No. It's just that before it was…spontaneous. This seems so—I don't know—premeditated."

"*Premeditated* is a word reserved for courtrooms and murder trials."

"You know what I mean."

"Yeah," he said, and heaved a disappointed sigh.

"I guess I do." He forced a smile and hugged her to his side. "There's nothing that says we have to use them tonight."

Unsure if she was relieved or disappointed that he'd accepted her reluctance so easily, she pushed slowly to her feet. "I guess I better get back to bed. It's late."

"Yeah, it is." He picked up the magazine he'd been reading and began to flip pages. "'Night, Leah."

Unsure why she suddenly had the wildest urge to snatch the magazine from his hand and bop him over the head with it, she mumbled a halfhearted "'Night, Sam" and turned for her room.

Leah couldn't blame her sleeplessness on worries over Craig any longer. Now it was Sam who was keeping her awake.

She flopped to her side and punched her pillow beneath her check, silently cursing him for telling her about the stupid condoms. If he'd kept quiet about his purchase, she wouldn't be thinking about him right now. Or sex, either, for that matter. She'd be asleep and not twisting and turning in frustration.

She heard a rustle of movement at the door and lifted her head. With the blinds shut tight to block the moonlight, the room was pitch-black, making it impossible for her to see so much as her hand in front of her face. She squinted hard, and her breath froze in her lungs when she saw a shadowed form moving across the room. She considered screaming, but before she could shape the sound, the sheet lifted and the shadow slipped into her bed. Though she still couldn't see, there was no mistaking the feel of the body that cuddled up against hers.

"Sam?" she whispered in disbelief.

His lips spread across hers in a smile. "Is this spontaneous enough for you?"

She wanted to laugh at his outrageousness, weep at his thoughtfulness in providing her the spontaneity she'd said was missing, but shivered instead as he slid his hands beneath the hem of her silk teddy.

Wrapping her arms around his neck, she said, "Perfect."

He stroked his hands slowly up and down her back as they kissed, and she shivered again as nerves danced to life along her spine.

Needing a connection, an anchor, she twined her legs with his and was shocked when her toes met bare skin. "You're naked," she said, wondering if he'd traipsed through her house in that state.

Smiling, he bumped his nose against hers. "You will be, too, in a minute."

Smoothing his hands up her back, he dragged her teddy up and over her head, dropped it over the side of the bed. He settled his hands at her waist. "Halfway there," he teased.

Laughing, she lifted her hips, making it easier for

him to peel off her tap pants, then snuggled close, weaving her legs through his again. "You're full of surprises tonight, Forrester."

"I may have one or two more up my sleeve." Lying opposite her, he cupped his hand around her breast. "If I remember correctly, your breasts are a turn-on for you."

He flicked a thumb over her nipple, and a low guttural moan slipped past her lips.

"Yeah," he murmured and dipped his head to catch the nipple between his teeth. Tugged. "That's the sound I remember."

Desire shot through her, piercing her belly, and spread to a deep, aching throb between her legs. "Oh, Sam," she groaned.

He opened his mouth over her breast and sucked her in. Weakened by the sensations that whipped through her, she filled her fingers with his hair and clung. "Oh, Sam."

He lifted his head and pressed his mouth to hers. "There you go again. Stretching my name into two syllables instead of one." He hitched himself higher on the bed. "Feel that?" he asked as he rocked his hips against hers. "That's what hearing you do that does to me."

Satin and steel. Those were the only two words she could think of to describe the feel of his erection rubbing against her groin. But then he slipped a hand between her legs and she lost all ability to think.

"You're hot," he whispered as he pushed a knuckle along her fold. "And wet."

She clamped her knees together, all but coming apart at his fingers' teasing. "Sam—" She swallowed, her mouth dry as dust, then wet her lips, prepared to beg if necessary.

He saved her that humiliation by sliding a hand down her thigh and drawing her leg up and over his. Anticipation quivered beneath her skin as he pushed his hips against hers, forcing himself between her legs. Every nerve in her body seemed centered on that one spot, tingling and burning with expectancy, with need. Closing her eyes, she arched her hips, and the tip of his shaft nudged her opening.

The pressure was so erotic, so unbelievably pleasurable that she arched again, a silent plea for more. "Sam," she whispered, barely recognizing her voice for the huskiness in it. "I want you. Now."

"Wait a sec."

She nearly screamed in frustration when he moved away and stretched to pluck something from the nightstand.

She heard the crinkle of foil and knew he was opening the condom package and rolling the protection into place.

"Okay," he said on a sigh and dragged her leg back over his. "Where were we?" Before she could tell him, he pressed his lips to hers and pushed inside, stealing her breath.

Jerking her mouth from his, she dropped her head back on a low moan as her body pulsed around him, then softened to accommodate him.

He moved his hips against hers, his shaft spearing deeper and deeper inside her with each slow thrust. Instinctively she followed his movements, meeting the rhythm he set and demanding a faster pace of her own.

Pressure built inside her, a smothering heat that slicked her skin, stripped much-needed oxygen from the air. She wanted to scream her frustration, beg for this moment to go on and on, weep at the glorious feel of him filling her so completely.

His breathing ragged, he closed a hand around her breast. She heard the low growl that built from deep inside him, felt the quiver of his legs against hers, the tension that strained his body, and gave herself up to the explosion of sensation that rocked through her body. Desperate to squeeze every nuance of pleasure from the experience, she grasped his buttocks in her hands and held him to her, letting him send her higher, higher still.

Like a leaf drifting in the wind, she floated slowly down, melting against him. She inhaled one deep, cleansing breath, then opened her eyes to find his gaze on hers. Awed by his rugged handsomeness as much as by what she'd just experienced, she touched a finger to his cheek to make sure she hadn't been dreaming. "Wow," she said, releasing the breath on a shuddery sigh.

Smiling, he brought her hand to his lips. "Yeah. Wow."

She snuggled close. "Tell me—do Boy Scouts have a badge for something like this?"

Chuckling, he shook his head. "I don't think so."

Pursing her lips in a sympathetic pout, she tucked her head in the curve of his shoulder. "That's too bad. You definitely would've earned yours."

Leah awakened slowly, vaguely aware of a slight soreness between her legs. Remembering the cause for the discomfort, she smiled and reached a hand out in search of Sam.

When her fingers met only cool sheets, she lifted her head and looked around. Finding herself alone, she dropped her head back to her pillow, telling herself it was best he'd left without waking her, saving them both the dreaded morning-after awkwardness.

In spite of her reassurance, tears of disappointment filled her eyes.

Refusing to give in to them, she threw back the covers and climbed from the bed. Just as she started down the stairs, she caught a whiff of what smelled like coffee brewing. Quickening her step, she hurried down the stairs and into the kitchen, where she found Sam standing before the stove.

"You're still here," she said in surprise.

He glanced over his shoulder, a brow lifted in question. "Was I supposed to leave?"

"No. No. It's just that…well, when I woke up and you weren't in bed, I assumed you'd gone back to the apartment."

Shaking his head, he turned his attention back to the stove. "It's that internal alarm clock of mine. It's set for five, and I've never figured out how to shut the dang thing off."

Relieved to know it wasn't regrets that had made him leave her, she crossed to see what he was cooking. "Pancakes?" she asked in surprise.

"Yep. Hungry?"

"Starving."

He shifted the spatula to his opposite hand and slid his arm around her waist. "Me, too. Guess we worked up a pretty good appetite last night, huh?"

Reminded of her almost insatiable desire for him, she blushed to the roots of her hair. "Yeah, I guess we did."

He dipped his head to nuzzle her ear. "I believe I could go another round or two without dying of hunger. How about you?"

She drew back to look at him, sure that he was teasing. When she saw the heat in his eyes, she melted against his chest with a smile. "I'm willing to chance it if you are."

Later that morning, Sam paused beneath the automotive store's awning to put on his sunglasses, thinking what a wild night of sex could do for a man's energy level. With only a couple of hours' sleep the night before, he felt as if he could wrestle a grizzly to the ground and make him cry uncle.

Chuckling, he stepped out onto the sidewalk but stopped again when a car full of teenagers pulled up at the red light, rap music blasting so loud the bass made his teeth ache.

"They'll be deaf before they hit thirty," he grumbled, then frowned when he saw a cigarette being passed around. "If they live that long."

With a woeful shake of his head, he started for the parking lot where he'd left his truck but stopped short and slowly turned back around, sure that he'd recognized one of the boys in the backseat.

"Craig?" he said, praying he was wrong.

Setting his jaw, he strode to the car and yanked open the rear door.

"Hey!" Craig cried and grabbed for the handle.

Sam stepped into the opening and bodily dragged the boy from the car.

"What do you think you're doing?" Craig cried, trying to wrench free. "Get your hands off me."

"Leave him alone," the driver of the car yelled.

Sam burned the driver with a look. "If you know what's good for you, you'll get the hell out of here before I call the cops and report you for truancy."

The kid must have believed him, because he peeled out before the other passenger in the backseat had time to shut the door.

Sam turned his anger on Craig. Seeing the cigarette that dangled from the boy's fingers, he snatched it from him and threw it down on the sidewalk. "Don't you know these things will kill you?" he said as he ground the cigarette out beneath his boot.

"Gonna die someday," Craig said arrogantly. "One way's as good as any other."

"If you believe that, you're dumber than you look."

"Are you calling me dumb?"

"I said you *look* dumb." Sam pointed a stiff finger at the crushed cigarette. "Especially when you're holding one of those." He narrowed an eye at Craig. "Aren't you supposed to be in school?"

Craig ducked his head, shrugged. "So I cut a few classes. Big deal."

"You're going to think big deal when your aunt finds out."

Craig snapped up his head, his eyes filled with dread. "You're gonna tell her?"

"Nope," Sam informed him. "You are." Taking the boy by the arm, he hustled him toward the truck. "But first you and I are going to pay a visit to your school principal."

Lying beneath the Mustang, Sam turned the wrench, tightening the last bolt on the new muffler he'd installed. Beyond him, the whirr of the lawn

mower's engine assured him that Craig hadn't gone
AWOL again.

The trip to the school had been an eye-opener for
Sam. He still couldn't believe the punishment for
skipping school these days was a few lousy hours
of detention. The one and only time he had cut
school, he'd gotten three licks for every class he'd
missed. Three *hard* licks delivered by the baseball
coach, who had spent some time in the minor
leagues and had the swing to prove it. Sam hadn't
been able to sit down for a week.

With a rueful shake of his head, he gave the
tailpipe a tug, testing its stability, then pushed his
boot heel against the drive and rolled the creeper
from beneath the car. Standing, he dragged a rag
from his back pocket and wiped his hands as he
watched Craig make another sweep around the
backyard. The lawn-mowing duty had been Sam's
idea, one he figured would keep the kid busy and out
of trouble until Leah got home from work.

And judging by the deep grooves that creased the
boy's forehead, it appeared Craig wasn't looking
forward to his aunt's arrival.

With a glance at his wristwatch, Sam decided to
call it a day and began picking up his tools. Though
it would have been a lot easier to leave everything
out, he'd made a few concessions in his work habits
in order to pacify Leah's concerns about him turning
her home into a junkyard. The first order of business

had been constructing a canopy over the car to shade it—and him—during the hottest portion of the day. Second on his list had been the placement of a tarpaulin beneath the car to protect the driveway from any oil and fluid spills. The last concession he'd come up with—actually a time-saver for him—was storing the most frequently used tools in the car's trunk.

And he hadn't made those concessions because he'd slept with Leah, he assured himself. It had simply taken him a while to figure out a compromise that would satisfy them both.

After depositing in the Mustang's trunk the tools he'd used that day, he stepped out into the yard to survey the work area he'd created. All in all, it wasn't too bad a setup, he decided. Leah would probably still consider it an eyesore, but she'd just have to deal. He'd done all he intended to do to appease what he considered her anal need for perfection.

Hearing a car door slam, he glanced over his shoulder and watched as Leah climbed from her SUV. He felt the stirring of desire in his groin and grinned, thinking of the night ahead.

She strode beneath the breezeway, her gaze fixed on the canopy. "Wow. Somebody's been busy."

Though he was a little disappointed she found the canopy more interesting than him, he turned to admire his handiwork. "You didn't want me working on the car out front, and I couldn't take the heat in the garage." He lifted a hand, indicating the canopy. "This is the compromise I came up with."

She walked around the perimeter of the structure, studying it closely. "You put this up by yourself?"

"Craig helped. He held the canvas in position while I secured it to the poles."

She looked at him in surprise. "*Craig* helped?"

"Yep." He nodded toward the backyard, where Craig was working. "He's mowing the yard, too."

She turned to peer at her nephew. "I can't believe this. I've asked him a zillion times to mow the yard and he always has an excuse." She glanced at Sam. "How in the world did you get him to do it?"

He buffed his nails on his chest and preened. "Oh, I have my ways."

"Well, don't be selfish. Share them with me. Nothing I've tried has ever worked."

Craig mowed the last strip and turned the mower toward the garage. When he spotted Leah standing with Sam, he stumbled a step, gulped, then pushed on, keeping his head down to avoid her gaze.

"Hi, Aunt Leah," he mumbled.

Smiling, she ruffled his hair. "Hi, yourself. And thanks for mowing the yard. I really appreciate it."

He lifted a shoulder. "No big deal."

"I'll put that away for you," Sam offered and took the mower from Craig. "You go on into the house with your aunt. I'm sure y'all have things to talk about."

His shoulders drooping, Craig nodded and turned for the house.

Leah looked at Sam in confusion. "What was that all about?"

"You'll find out soon enough."

Leah tried her best to keep her anger in check as she listened to Craig's explanation. When he finished, she sat in silence for a long moment, unsure what to say for fear whatever she said would distance her nephew even further.

"Does your mother know about this?" she asked.

"No. Just you. And Sam."

She curled her hand into a fist in her lap, curbing the desire to comb his hair back from his eyes so she could see his face.

"You said that Sam took you to see the principal."

"Yeah," he muttered sourly. "I got slammed with two weeks of detention."

A mild punishment, in her estimation, but she wasn't about to share her opinion with Craig.

"When do you begin serving them?"

"Monday. Seven-thirty to eight-thirty every day for two whole weeks."

She firmed her lips at his resentful tone. "Ten hours spent studying certainly won't hurt your grades any."

He tucked his chin closer to his chest at the mention of his downward-spiraling grades.

A horn beeped outside, and Leah glanced toward the front of the house, knowing it was Patrice. She turned to face Craig again. "Are you going to tell your mom about this?"

He lifted a shoulder, dropped it. "She's so wigged-out all the time, she probably wouldn't even hear me if I did."

Leah made a decision that she hoped wouldn't come back to haunt her. Reaching across the table, she covered her nephew's hand with her own. "Let's just keep this between us for now."

"Whatever."

The horn beeped again and Craig dragged himself to his feet. "I better go." He hitched his backpack over his shoulder and turned to leave.

In the doorway he hesitated a moment, and she held her breath, praying that he'd say *I'm sorry* or something that would indicate he regretted what he'd done. But he stepped outside, letting the door close behind him, without uttering a word.

Leah watched him leave, her heart breaking. He looked so much like Kevin had at that age. Legs too long for his body. Hair long and shaggy. Eyes that harbored a sadness that nothing could reach. Like his father, Craig had no mother to turn to for comfort and reassurance. In her own way, Patrice was as oblivious to her son's needs as Leah and Kevin's mother had been to theirs.

Tears filled her throat and she dropped her forehead to her folded arms, willing them back. Crying wouldn't bring Kevin back or absolve her fears for Craig. She'd shed enough over the years to know they were nothing but a waste of time.

"Leah?"

She lifted her head and found Sam standing in the doorway. She quickly scraped her hands across her cheeks and rose, not wanting him to see that she'd been crying. "Craig told me what happened this morning."

His expression somber, he stepped inside. "I was hoping he would."

She had the most irresistible urge to bury her face against his chest and sob. To keep herself from giving into it, she turned for the refrigerator. "I appreciate what you did for him. Taking him back to school and making him tell the principal what he'd done."

"Facing the music is always hard. Figured he might need a little encouragement."

She pulled a pitcher of lemonade from the refrigerator, her smile wistful as she closed the door. "Encouragement is something he's short on right now."

"He has you," he reminded her.

Shaking her head, she took two glasses from the cabinet. "I'm not enough. I can't reach him any more. He needs is his father." Feeling the tears rising again, she firmed her lips and focused her attention on filling the glasses. Turning, she forced a smile and offered one to Sam. "How about some lemonade?"

He accepted the glass. "Thanks."

She gestured toward the sunroom. "Let's sit out there."

She led the way, with Sam following, and settled in a wicker chair.

He took the chair next to hers.

"Craig tells me that you and the principal have an agreement to keep Patrice on a need-to-know basis only."

She nodded. "Patrice is…fragile. I handle whatever problems arise at school to save her the additional stress."

"Do you mind if I ask you a question?"

She stole a glance his way. "That depends on the question."

"Why do you avoid talking about your brother?"

Blanching, she looked away, not wanting to share her reasons. "I'd think that would be obvious."

"If you mean grief, that I can understand. It's hard losing someone you love. But I think it's more than just grief."

Pursing her lips, she swept a drop of condensation impatiently from her glass. "You can think whatever you like."

"Leah?"

When she refused to look at him, he laid a hand over hers.

"Leah, look at me."

Though she'd have preferred to look anywhere other than at him, she met his gaze. The compassion she found in his eyes nearly brought her to her knees.

"You're mad, aren't you?" he said quietly.

She felt the sting of tears and blinked them back. "Why would I be mad at you?" she asked, purposely misunderstanding his question.

"Not me. Your brother."

The tears surged higher, a wall of emotion that blocked any hope she might have had of denying his assumption a second time.

Before she realized his intention, he had tugged her from her chair and onto his lap.

"Ah, Leah," he said miserably. He tucked her head beneath his chin and pressed a kiss on top of her head. "I'm not Craig or Patrice. You don't have to keep up a brave front for me. I won't think any less of you for admitting that you're angry with Kevin for dying."

She gulped but couldn't hold back the emotion that choked her. She turned her face against his neck. "He didn't have to die," she sobbed miserably. "He could've stayed home with his family. With me."

He stroked a hand over her hair. "Soldiers aren't given a choice," he reminded her. "They go where they're sent, where their country needs them."

She shook her head. "He never should have

enlisted. He was barely eighteen. Too young to know what he was doing or what he wanted to do with his life. He only did it because of Mom."

"Your mother asked him to enlist?" he asked in confusion.

"No. He did it to get her attention. Maybe to spite her. I don't know." She squeezed her eyes shut, remembering the hours she'd spent pleading with him not to join the Army. "I begged him not to do it, told him that it wouldn't make any difference, that Mom was never going to change no matter what either of us did. But he wouldn't listen. It was like he needed to prove something. Or maybe get even with her for ignoring him."

Hitching a breath, she pressed a hand against her lips and shook her head. "I don't know. But no matter how much I screamed and begged, I couldn't get through to him. And Mom—she was oblivious. Didn't say a word to him. Just kept on with her stupid research, as if Kevin wasn't making the biggest mistake of his life."

"I take it you've always been the one in charge, looking out for your mother and brother."

She swiped at her cheeks. "Somebody had to, and Mom couldn't or wouldn't."

"And now you're looking out for Craig and Patrice."

She lifted her head, shot a hand beneath her nose. "I have to. Kevin's not here to take care of them."

"And who takes care of Leah?" he asked softly.

She stared, then turned her face away, unable to meet his gaze.

He placed a hand on her cheek and turned her face back to his. "Who?" he prodded.

She stared, her lip quivering, thinking of all the times she'd wanted someone to lean on, someone to help carry the burden for a while. She'd hoped, prayed, that Louis would be that someone. Instead he'd ridiculed her concern for her family, refused to spend any holidays in their company and done everything he could to distance her from them.

Jutting her chin, she shoved his hand away. "I don't need anyone to take care of me. I can take care of myself."

"Everybody needs somebody."

She pushed from his lap. "Well, I don't. And if you think my sleeping with you gives you the right to interfere in my life, you're wrong."

Five

Sam stood with a shoulder braced against the doorjamb of the apartment, his arms folded across his chest, looking up at the night sky. To say he was frustrated would be the understatement of the year. He'd thought he'd be sharing Leah's bed again tonight, but the conversation they'd had in the sunroom had nixed any chance of that happening.

But sex wasn't the cause of his frustration. Not solely, anyway. He was worried about Leah. He was afraid if somebody didn't do something, and soon, she was going to crumple beneath the weight of the family responsibilities she carried. Granted, her sense of duty to Craig and Patrice was admirable, but Sam was a firm believer in the teach-a-person-to-fish approach to dealing with problems. In his opinion, as long as Leah continued to take care of Craig and Patrice, they would never step up to the plate and assume responsibility for their own emotional and physical needs. They'd continue to drain Leah until she had nothing left to give them.

He wanted to help her. If nothing else, to offer her some much-needed support. But every time he tried, the damn fool woman stiff-armed him, insisting she could take care of herself, just as she had that afternoon.

He supposed he could understand her obstinance. She'd been taking care of herself and those around her so long it had probably become a habit, one she couldn't break.

But he was convinced there was something more behind her stubborn refusal to accept help from anyone…and he had a sneaky suspicion it stemmed from her mother's suicide. He remembered when she'd told him about her mother's obsession with finding her father, Leah saying he probably thought her mother was crazy, the same as everyone else in town. Reason enough for her to refuse offers of help from outsiders, as she wouldn't want to subject her family to more public scorn.

But it wasn't reason enough to refuse Sam's.

In his mind, her refusal represented a lack of

trust. And that irritated the hell out of him, as trust was a trait he valued and strived hard to earn.

He'd never given her any reason to distrust him, he told himself. He had a key to her house, yet he'd never once taken advantage of that privilege. He bought his own groceries and what other necessities he needed and was careful to always replace what items of hers he used. He even helped out around the house, emptying the dishwasher when it needed it, sweeping the kitchen floor the few times he'd tracked dirt inside. And he'd started cleaning the pool, figuring it was the least he could do, since she allowed him to use it. He even helped her keep an eye on Craig.

You didn't tell her you were in the Army.

He flinched at his conscience's prodding, then squared his shoulders. And for good reason, he thought defensively. Leah blamed the Army for the loss of her father and brother. She'd made it clear from the get-go that she wanted nothing to do with anyone associated with the military. If he'd told her he currently served with Special Forces, he would've lost any chance he had of getting the information he'd promised Mack.

Leading her to believe you were a mechanic who'd come to apply for the job of restoring the car is the same as lying, which is reason enough to earn her distrust.

It's not the same, he argued stubbornly. He'd never out-and-out lied to her.

He just hadn't given her the whole truth.

He rolled his shoulders, trying to shake free from the guilt his conscience was piling on him, but it stuck like glue, refusing to budge.

With a resigned sigh, he glanced toward Leah's darkened bedroom window and wondered if she was having trouble sleeping, too. He could imagine her there, tossing and turning, worrying about Craig, grieving for her brother. He wanted to go to her, share her burden, offer what comfort he could, but knew he'd only alienate her more if he did.

Maybe he ought to come clean, he told himself. Tell her the truth about who he was and why he was at her house. She'd be madder than a hornet, there was no question about that. But surely after she'd cooled down she'd understand, perhaps even admire his determination to honor his promise to Mack, sympathize with his need to provide his friend's wife with another piece of the puzzle to her father's life. Once she realized the honorableness of his mission, she'd give him the piece of paper he wanted and he could be on his way, putting her and her family's problems behind him.

His gaze fixed on her window, he realized that leaving was no longer an option. He couldn't walk away from Leah when he knew how badly she needed help. Not only in restoring her brother's car but with her nephew, too. The boy was headed for trouble, a place Sam was all too familiar with. What the kid needed was guidance, a firm hand, the influence only a man could provide a young, impressionable boy quickly approaching adulthood.

And Leah needed Sam. She'd never admit it, might not even be aware of the lack in her life. But he was. She was haunted by her father's and brother's deaths, possibly even her mother's, and had devoted her life to protecting her nephew and sister-in-law from any more hurt.

She deserved a life of her own, one free of obligation and responsibility to others. But she'd never know any true peace, any happiness, until she stopped avoiding her past and dealt with it once and for all.

And when she did that, she was going to need someone to lean on, someone to comfort her, lend her strength.

And Sam intended to be that someone.

The overhead light snapped on, yanking Leah bolt upright in bed.

Sam stood in the doorway, his hand on the switch.

"What are you doing?" she cried.

He flipped off the light and started across the room. "Seeing if you were awake."

He stopped beside the bed, and though it was dark, his movements were clear enough for her to know he was stripping off his sweatpants.

"Just because I slept with you once," she said

angrily, "doesn't give you the right to march into my bedroom anytime you want."

"I'm not here for sex."

She blinked, taken aback, then set her jaw. "Then why are you here?"

He lifted the sheet and slid into bed beside her. "Couldn't sleep. You really should get a new mattress for the apartment."

"There's nothing wrong with that mattress!" she cried indignantly.

"For Fred Flintstone, maybe. It's like lying on a slab of stone."

"You never complained before."

He tugged her down to lie beside him and settled his head next to hers on the pillow. "Wasn't aware of the difference until I slept in yours."

"Sam," she warned when he hooked an arm over her waist and cuddled close.

"Shh." He closed his eyes. "You need to get some sleep. We both do."

Leah wanted to argue, but he began to stroke his hand up and down her back, distracting her. She waited, convinced that any second he'd give up the ruse and attempt to seduce her and she could kick him out of her room for the liar he was.

But with each slow glide of his hand more and more of the tension melted from her back and her eyelids grew heavy. Heavier still.

She slept, lulled by the rhythmic sound of Sam's breathing.

* * *

Leah opened her eyes, startled awake by the sound of a car on the drive. It took her a moment to associate the unusual warmth at her back and the weight that pinned her legs with Sam. She started to close her eyes and snuggle back against the warmth but flipped them wide when she heard a car door open and slam.

Throwing back the covers, she ran to the window and lifted a slat to peek through the blinds.

"Oh, no!" Whirling, she cried, "You've got to get out of here!"

Sam pulled the pillow over his head. "It's Saturday," he mumbled. "Come back to bed."

She snatched the pillow from his head. "Patrice just dropped Craig off. You've got to get out of here."

He blinked up at her, his hair tousled from sleep. "Why?"

"He can't find us in bed together! What would he think?"

"That we were tired?" he asked hopefully.

She flattened her lips. "Sa-am…"

He knew by the warning she placed in the two-syllable pronunciation of his name that she wasn't making the distinction because she was aroused. He also knew he wasn't getting any more sleep.

"Okay, okay," he grumbled as he rolled from the bed. He scooped his sweatpants from the floor and tugged them on as he headed for the door. "I'll go downstairs and intercept him."

"Dressed like that?" she cried. "You can't! He'll know the minute he sees you that you spent the night." She worried her thumbnail, trying to think of a plausible explanation. "Tell him I saw a mouse. Yeah, a mouse," she said, liking the idea. "And I called you to come and catch it for me."

He looked down his nose at her. "Do you really think he's going to fall for a cock-and-bull story like that?"

She gave him a push. "He will if you make it sound convincing."

Shaking his head, he jogged down the stairs, leaving her to dress. When he entered the kitchen, Craig was pouring cereal into a bowl.

"Hey, Craig," he said. "I didn't know you were coming over today."

Craig looked up. He glanced in the direction Sam had appeared, then back at Sam. "What are you doing here?" he asked suspiciously.

Rolling his eyes, Sam crossed to the refrigerator and pulled out a jug of orange juice. "Your aunt saw a mouse. Called me, all hysterical, begging me to come and catch it for her."

Craig's expression remained dubious. "So where's the mouse?"

Sam snorted as he poured orange juice into a

glass. "You ever known a person who caught a mouse with his bare hands?"

Craig smothered a laugh. "No."

"Me either," Sam replied and took a swig of juice. Backhanding the moisture from his mouth, he dragged out a chair and swung it around, straddling it as he sat opposite Craig at the table. "Women. Nothing but a bunch of sissies. Guess this means I'll be making a run to the store for a mousetrap."

"Yeah. Looks like it."

"Want to go with me?"

"I guess."

Leah breezed into the kitchen wearing an over-bright smile and a T-shirt turned wrong-side out. "Morning, Craig. I suppose Sam told you about the mouse?"

He glanced up, then ducked his head and scooped up a spoonful of cereal. "Yeah. He told me."

Sam ducked his head, too, deciding it might not be the best time to tell Leah about her wardrobe blunder.

Oblivious to their amusement—or her state of dress—Leah pulled a bowl from the cabinet. "I didn't know you were planning on coming over today," she said to Craig.

"Wasn't. Mom's having one of her…spells."

Leah's face crumpled. "Oh, honey," she said sympathetically and draped an arm around her nephew's shoulders. "I'm so sorry."

Craig shrugged. "No big deal. I'll just hang out here till she settles down."

Nodding, Leah seated herself at the table and reached for the cereal box. "Maybe you and Sam can work on the car," she suggested hopefully.

Craig peeked at Sam from beneath his mass of bangs. "Maybe," he said, hiding a smile. "But we gotta buy a mousetrap, first. Right, Sam?"

Craig stood beside Sam, holding the wing nut, while Sam fitted the cover back over the carburetor.

"You spent the night with Aunt Leah, didn't you?"

The question came out of nowhere and had Sam fumbling the cover. He straightened slowly and pulled off his ball cap to drag an arm across the sweat on his brow. "Yeah, I did," he admitted reluctantly.

"So why did y'all make up that crazy story about the mouse?"

Sam puffed his cheeks and blew out a breath, knowing he was treading on thin ice. Slinging an arm around Craig's shoulders, he guided him toward a bench beneath a tree. "Because your aunt didn't want to give you the wrong impression."

Craig flopped down on the bench and peered up at Sam. "What? That she sleeps around?"

Since Sam couldn't see Craig's eyes, he didn't know whether the kid was being serious or a wiseass. Frustrated, he shot a hand through the boy's hair and slapped his ball cap over the top of his head.

Craig threw up his hands. "Hey!" he cried, trying to duck. "What are you doing?"

Sam tugged the cap down, pinning the boy's hair beneath it, then stooped and put his face level with Craig's. "Getting your hair out of your eyes," he informed him. "That's what. When I talk to a person, I want to see his eyes."

Craig spun the cap around, placing the bill in the back. "What's the big deal about seeing a person's eyes?" he grumbled.

Sam dropped down on the bench beside him with a sigh. "Because eyes don't lie. If you want to know what a person is thinking, you've got to be able to look them square in the eyes."

"That's bull."

"Think so?" Sam challenged. He turned his back to Craig. "I've never been in jail in my life," he said, then faced Craig again, careful to keep his expression blank. "Was I lying or telling the truth?"

Frowning, Craig studied him closely for a moment. "The truth."

Sam fixed his gaze on Craig's. "Keep your eyes on mine and let's try that again. By the time I was eighteen I'd been thrown in jail a minimum of six times." He sank back and braced his spine on the trunk of the tree. "So? Truth or lie?"

Craig's eyes rounded. "Holy smoke. You've really been in jail that many times?"

"Yeah," Sam admitted reluctantly, then gave Craig a stern look. "And I didn't use that example because I'm proud of my past. It was only to make a point." He jerked up his chin, indicating the cap. "People who keep their eyes hidden are hiding something else, too—usually the truth. If you want a person to believe you, you've got to look him straight in the eye."

Craig tugged the cap off, combed his hair back over his forehead and pulled the cap over his head again. "Even more reason to keep my hair in my eyes. Nobody'll ever know when I'm lying."

"Oh, they'll find out eventually," Sam informed him. "A man's lies catch up with him sooner or later. But you're missing the point. You can't trust what a man tells you unless you can look him square in the eye." He waited a beat, then said, "And your aunt does *not* sleep around."

Grimacing, Craig dragged off the cap and shoved his hair beneath it again. "I know that."

"Well, I want to make damn sure you do. Your aunt's a nice woman. A lady. And I won't have you thinking or saying bad things about her."

Craig cast him a sideways look. "You like her?"

Though he wasn't ready to share his newly discovered feelings for Leah just yet, Sam kept his gaze fixed on Craig's, knowing—after the lecture he'd just delivered—to look away would be a mistake. "Yeah, I do. You got a problem with that?"

Craig shrugged. "That's cool with me. Aunt Leah hasn't had a boyfriend since she divorced Louis the Loser."

Sam choked a laugh. "Louis the Loser?"

Craig scowled. "That's her ex. I never liked him. Nobody did."

"Your Aunt Leah must have. She married him."

His scowl deepened. "She might've married him, but I don't think she liked him all that much."

Sam knew it was wrong to press the kid for details, but he wasn't about to let an opportunity like this pass. "If she didn't like him, why'd she marry him?"

Craig bent over and picked up a twig from the ground. "I heard my dad tell my mom she married him for his money."

Sam had a hard time swallowing that line of reasoning. Leah didn't seem the type who'd trade her freedom and her heart for a bank account, no matter how many zeros followed the dollar sign. "Do you think that's why she did it?"

His gaze on the twig he spun between his fingers, Craig shook his head. "Nah. Aunt Leah's no gold digger."

"Then why do you think she married the guy?"

Craig lifted his head and looked at Sam. "Because she wanted somebody to love and thought he'd love her back."

There was no questioning the sincerity in the boy's eyes. "And he didn't?"

Scowling, Craig reared back and threw the twig as far as he could. "Louis the Loser loves one person. Himself. Aunt Leah was nothing but a game to him. She's pretty, smart, built her business up all by herself. Every single guy in town was chasing her, so Louis did a snow job on her. Bought her presents all the time, took her nice places, acted like she was the only woman in the whole universe. Made her feel special. Loved."

"I take it once they were married he quit treating her that way."

Craig snorted. "He was screwing around on her the day they got back from their honeymoon."

Sam gave him a doubtful look. "You don't know that for sure."

"Yeah, I do." Craig rose and started for the car. "Aunt Leah knew it, too," he called over his shoulder. "She caught him coming out of a motel room with some woman. Cried for days."

Sam couldn't shake free of the image Craig had planted in his mind of Leah crying for days after catching her husband in a compromising position.

If what Craig had said was true, then Leah must have loved Louis despite her nephew's insistence that she hadn't liked the man. Why else would she have cried when she'd caught him cheating on her?

Didn't matter, Sam told himself as he dragged the skimmer over the pool's surface. Whether Leah loved Louis or not, that was all in the past. It was the now that concerned him. Specifically Leah's now.

He'd learned some other things from Craig—turned out the kid was a real Chatty Cathy once a person got him talking. Through carefully phrased probing, Sam had discovered that the boy knew almost nothing about his grandfather. According to Craig, his grandfather's name was taboo with everyone except his grandmother, and she was so "weirded out," as Craig had described her, that he'd learned not to mention his grandfather's name in front of her, either.

Another item of interest he'd gleaned from the kid was the fact that Leah and her brother had grown up in near poverty. Amazing, considering her current digs and her obsession for neatness and order.

Or maybe that explained why she was the way she was, he realized slowly.

Growing thoughtful, he dragged the net across the pool's surface, scooping up leaves. When he added to the equation the fact that Leah was raised by a present-in-body-only mother, it made sense that she would strive to make up for all that was lacking in her youth.

It also explained how she'd developed her mother-hen tendency toward her family.

As the oldest, she more than likely would have assumed the responsibilities her mother shirked, including watching out for her little brother, a responsibility she'd carried with her into adulthood. And when "little brother" died, leaving a widow and orphaned son behind, she'd spread her mother-hen wings a little wider and drawn his family close, assuming the role of their protector.

Oh, yeah, he thought in satisfaction as he dumped the waterlogged leaves into the trash can. He had figured out the whys and why-fors behind Ms. Leah Kittrell's personality quirks.

Now he just had to figure out how to put the information to use to free her from her past.

The most likely place to start seemed to be with her father, since her father's classification as MIA seemed to be the point when the family began to fall apart. If he could somehow manage to dispel the mystery surrounding her father's death, he could give Leah the closure she needed, which would allow her to begin healing other areas of her life.

And he knew just the man to call to assist him in uncovering the information he'd need to give her that closure.

Pulling out his cell phone, he punched in a number, then waited through two rings.

"Hey, Jack," he said to the man who answered. "It's Sam. How're you doing?"

He laughed at Jack's sarcastic response, then said,

"Listen, buddy. I need a favor. I have a friend whose father was listed as MIA in Vietnam. Jessie Kittrell, from Texas. I need you to find out what you can about him. Where he was last seen, any intelligence that mentions him or other soldiers from his unit, who were listed as MIA at the same time—that kind of thing."

Scrunching up his nose, he scratched his head as he listened to Jack's grumbled complaints. "Yeah, I know it's not much to go on, but that's all I've got."

He listened again, then grinned. "I knew I could count on you, buddy. I owe you one."

Pleased to have made a step in the right direction, he slipped his cell phone back into its holster at his waist and picked up the pool net again.

"You don't have to do that."

He jumped at the sound of Leah's voice, then turned, praying she hadn't overheard his conversation. "Only fair. I use it as much as you." Noticing that she was wearing a business suit, he looked at her in puzzlement. "It's Saturday. Why are you dressed for work?"

"I have a committee meeting." She stepped out onto the patio. "I wanted to thank you before I left."

"You don't owe me any thanks. Like I said, it's only fair since I use the pool, too."

She shook her head. "No, I meant for spending the day with Craig. He needed the distraction. When Patrice gets likes this, it upsets him."

He nodded soberly. "Yeah, I imagine it does."

She dropped her chin, as if she had something else to say but was having a hard time getting the words out.

"About last night…" she began.

"What about it?" he prodded.

She lifted her head and met his gaze. "I'm sorry for the things I said. I don't want you to think I don't appreciate your kindness to me. It's just that…" She drew in a deep breath. "I don't like people telling me how to handle my family."

"That wasn't my intent. I just wanted to help is all. It seems you're carrying an awful heavy load."

"They're my family. All I've got. I'd do anything for them."

"Yeah. I imagine you would."

She hesitated a moment. "I want to thank you for sleeping with me, too." She dropped her chin, a blush staining her cheeks. "I know how stupid that sounds. How childish. But it was comforting to know that you were there, that I wasn't alone."

"Leah—" he began.

She looked at her watch. "I really need to go. I'm already late."

"Is it a dinner meeting?" he asked.

She shook her head. "Strictly business."

"How about I cook tonight? Something on the grill."

Her eyes brightened. "Are you serious?"

"As a heart attack."

A slow smile spread across her face. "Well, yeah. That would be great. I should be through by seven-thirty, eight at the latest."

"Come home hungry."

Steaks flame-broiled over mesquite wood. A bottle of Chianti wine. A table set for two beneath a moonlit sky. Roses scenting the night air.

Sam had planned the evening down the last detail, wanting to give Leah a relaxing, stress-free evening…or was he trying to prove to her that he could be as charming as her ex?

Grimacing, he lowered the lid over the grill, silently cursing Craig for telling him about Louis the Loser and the damn snow job he'd done on Leah to persuade her to marry him.

This wasn't a competition, he told himself. He wasn't trying to outromance Louis the Loser. And he wasn't interested in marriage. He just wanted to give Leah something she seldom, if ever, enjoyed. A night free from worry, even those associated with preparing a meal.

"Wow."

He turned, and his heart shifted in his chest when he saw Leah poised on the steps of the house. She still wore her business suit but had removed the jacket. But she could've had on worn-out sweats and looked just as beautiful to

Sam. A woman couldn't hide that kind of beauty even if she'd tried.

She started toward him but stopped to examine the table he'd set and lifted a brow. "China?"

"Only the best for the owner of Stylized Events."

"You didn't have to go to so much trouble," she scolded as she crossed to him. She rose to her toes and placed a kiss on his cheek. "But it's lovely." She braced a hand against his chest and looked around. "Everything is."

He lifted the dome on the grill to check the steaks. "Ten minutes," he reported and closed the lid. "How about a glass of wine?"

"I wouldn't turn one down."

He poured two glasses, passed her one. "How was your meeting?"

"Boring."

He hid a smile behind the rim of his glass as he watched her rearrange the silverware beside the plates. "I guess I must've missed the etiquette class on proper table settings."

She snatched her hand behind her back. "Sorry," she said, wincing. "Habit."

He chuckled as he pulled out a chair for her. "Considering your line of business, I'd imagine it's more than habit."

She looked up at him over her shoulder as she sat down. "I hate to sound ungrateful, but—" she spread her hands "—what's all this about?"

He seated himself across the table from her. "No reason. Just thought you could stand some spoiling."

She picked up the rose he'd placed across her plate and lifted it to her nose. She closed her eyes as she inhaled its fragrance, then smiled and tucked it behind her ear. "I definitely rate this as spoiling. I can't remember the last time anyone went to this much trouble for me."

He lifted his glass. "Even more reason for you to enjoy it."

Bracing her arms against the table, she leaned to study him from across the table. "I can't figure you out. One minute I want to strangle you and the next I want to bottle you so that every woman can enjoy your sweetness."

"Sweet? Me?" Laughing, he shook his head. "I've been called a lot of things in my lifetime, but 'sweet' was never one of them."

"But you are," she insisted. "And thoughtful and kind and generous, too."

His smile soft, he braced his arms on the table, mimicking her posture. "You just described yourself."

She stared, then pushed out a hand, laughing. "See? I'm trying to pay you a compliment and you won't accept it."

"Right back at you."

Holding up her hands, she sank back in her chair. "Okay, I give up. You're incorrigible and impossible."

He smiled proudly. "Now you're talking." He glanced at his watch and pushed from his chair. "Steaks should be about ready. Hungry?"

"Starved. What can I do to help?"

"I made salad. It's in the refrigerator, if you don't mind getting it."

She scraped back her chair. "Anything else?"

He shook his head as he lifted the lid. "I've got everything else right here on the grill."

"Sam?"

He glanced over his shoulder. "Yeah?"

"You really are sweet."

Sweet.

Sam glanced back at the bed where Leah slept and shook his head. She wouldn't think he was so sweet if she knew the truth about him.

Heaving a sigh, he turned to stare out the window again. Telling a couple of half-truths shouldn't bother a man who lived a life of subterfuge and espionage, but the duplicity surrounding his relationship with Leah was beginning to wear on his nerves.

He knew he couldn't keep up the charade much longer. Not when he'd grown to care for her. He stopped, considering the thought, then slowly relaxed. It was true—he did care for her, was possibly even falling in love with her.

He frowned again. But that in itself made it even more important for him to tell her who he was and what he was doing at her house. He'd planned to come clean earlier, after dinner, but the timing just hadn't seemed right. She had been so pleased with the dinner he'd cooked for her, so happy and relaxed, he'd hated to ruin it all just to free himself of guilt.

"Sam?"

He whipped his head around to find Leah propped on an elbow, her forehead pleated in concern.

"Are you okay?" she asked.

Smiling softly, he returned to the bed. "I'm fine." He hooked an arm over her waist and settled his head on the pillow opposite hers. "Couldn't sleep. Probably ate too much."

Her smile sleepy, she nuzzled her cheek against his chest. "I'd have thought we worked off that meal."

Chuckling at the reminder of the amount of time they'd spent at sexual aerobics, he pressed his lips against her hair. "We gave it our best shot, that's for damn sure."

She placed a hand over his heart and closed her eyes. "Go to sleep," she murmured. "Morning will be here soon."

The tenderness of her touch seemed to burn through his chest and wrap around his heart. Closing his eyes against the ache that swelled there, he buried his nose in her hair and drank in her scent.

And wondered if she'd still be willing to share her bed with him once he told her the truth.

Six

Sam strained to fit the new battery beneath the Mustang's hood. After only three weeks of mildly intense labor he was close to getting this little baby running.

"Hey, Sam!"

He glanced up and had to do a double take to make sure it was Craig who was jogging up the drive.

He gave the battery a last shove, clicking it into position on its frame, then hitched his hands on his hips. "Well, look at you. What happened? Get your head caught in a fan?"

Breathless from running, Craig dumped his backpack on the drive. "Got a haircut."

Sam circled him, admiring the shorter style.

"Damn if you aren't pretty. Who'd have guessed there was a face under all that hair?"

Blushing, Craig ducked his head. "Cut it out. It's just a haircut."

Chuckling, Sam scrubbed his knuckles over Craig's head. "This calls for a celebration. Shakes on me."

Craig's face lit up. "Cool! Can I drive?"

Sam crossed to his truck and opened the passenger door. "Do you have a license?"

"Come on, Sam. You know I don't."

"Guess that means I'll be doing the driving."

Grimacing, Craig climbed into the cab.

"How am I ever going to learn to drive," he complained as Sam slid behind the wheel, "when nobody'll ever let me?"

"There's a time and place for everything," Sam informed him as he started the engine. "And city streets aren't the place for driving lessons." He put the truck into gear. "That's what country roads were made for. Know any?"

Craig's eyes widened. "Does that mean you'll teach me?"

"If you know a remote road we can use."

"Out by the lake. There's millions out there and people hardly ever use 'em."

"The lake it is, then," Sam said, then glanced at Craig. "Unless you still want that shake."

"Heck no! I want to *drive!*"

With Craig serving as his navigational director, Sam located a remote country road perfect for giving a teenager his first turn behind the wheel.

After pulling onto the shoulder and switching off the ignition, he said to Craig, "Okay. So tell me how much experience you've had at driving."

Craig scrunched up his nose. "Not much. Aunt Leah has let me drive her SUV a couple of times."

"Then you know the basics. Accelerator, brake, that kind of thing?"

"Yeah." Craig studied the controls on the dash behind the steering wheel. "Everything looks pretty much the same as on Aunt Leah's."

Sam opened his door. "Then let's get this show on the road."

While he rounded the hood, Craig climbed over the console and dropped down behind the wheel. By the time Sam settled into the passenger seat, Craig had touched and tested every dial on the dash, including the radio.

Grimacing, Sam turned down the volume. "You'll need to adjust the seat," he instructed. "Controls are on the left-hand side. Push the longest to move the seat forward or back. The shortest up or down to adjust the seat's height."

"Right." His forehead pleated in concentration, Craig pressed a button. The seat moved forward a couple of inches, then stopped, and the motor began to grind.

He yanked his hand off the button and looked at Sam in alarm. "Did I do something wrong?"

Amused by the kid's fear, he shook his head. "Probably something caught on the glide blocking it and keeping the seat from moving. Reach underneath and see if you feel anything."

Craig groped a minute, then shook his head. "Can't reach that far."

"Then you're going to have to get out and look."

Craig opened the door, hopped down, then bent over and peered beneath the seat.

"I see something," he said and stuck his arm under the seat, straining to reach it. "Got it!" he exclaimed and pulled out a metal box.

Sam swallowed a groan when he saw the olive-green box, with *Property of Sam Forrester, U.S. Army, Special Forces* emblazoned across the lid.

"What's this?" Craig asked in puzzlement.

Sam stretched across the seat and snatched the box from the boy's hand. "Just some old papers," he said vaguely and stuffed the box under the passenger seat and out of sight.

Frowning, Craig climbed back into the truck and shut the door.

Sam pasted on a smile. "Okay, hot rod. Give her a whirl."

Craig turned the key, starting the engine. He started to pull down the gearshift, but dropped his hand and turned to look at Sam. "You're in the Army, aren't you?"

Sam silently cursed his own stupidity for not remembering that he'd stuck the box with his paperwork beneath the seat. "Yeah," he admitted reluctantly.

"Does Aunt Leah know?"

He shook his head. "I thought it best not to mention it, considering how she feels about the military."

"She's going to be majorly P.O.'d when she finds out."

Sam heaved a sigh. "Yeah, I know." He hesitated a moment, then said, "Listen, Craig. I'd appreciate it if you wouldn't say anything about this. I'd prefer to tell her myself."

"Why'd you lie to her in the first place?"

"I didn't lie," Sam said defensively. When Craig merely looked at him, he scowled. "I didn't lie," he said stubbornly. "I just didn't tell her the whole truth."

"Which is…?" Craig prodded.

Sam gave him a long look, knowing he was going to have to tell the kid the whole story. How could he do any less when he'd been preaching truth and honesty to the kid?

"I'm not a mechanic," he admitted. "At least not professionally. I'm a lieutenant in the United States Army, currently assigned to Special Forces."

Craig's eyes rounded. "You're a Green Beret?"

"Yeah, I am." He peered at Craig closely. "Do you have a problem with that?"

"Heck, no. Green Berets are awesome. They're like superninjas. They can do anything."

Chuckling, Sam shook his head. "Not quite everything."

"Aunt Leah's gonna blow a gasket, though. She hates the Army."

"Yeah, I know," Sam said miserably.

"So when are you going to tell her?"

Sam turned his face to the passenger window. "Soon," he promised. "Just waiting on the right time."

"I'll go with you to tell her if you want."

Sam glanced at the kid, surprised by the offer. "You'd do that?"

Craig shrugged. "Only fair. You went to the principal's office with me."

Leah grabbed Craig's face and held it between her hands. "Just look at you! You cut off all your hair!"

Scowling, he wriggled free. "Yeah. Mom took me to the barbershop yesterday. Guess what?" he said, his face brightening.

"What?"

"I drove Sam's truck."

"You *what?*" she cried, then looked at Sam for confirmation.

He shrugged. "Country road. No traffic. It was safe."

"And I didn't wreck it or anything," Craig said proudly.

Leah sputtered a laugh. "Well, thank heaven for that."

He turned to Sam, his face flushed with excitement. "How long before you think the Mustang's ready to drive?"

"Couple of days. By the weekend at the latest."

Leah's stomach knotted, realizing what that meant. Once the Mustang was finished, there would be no reason for Sam to stay.

Numbed by the thought, she turned away. "I don't know that you're ready for the Mustang just yet," she said to Craig.

"Sure I am! Tell her, Sam. I drove really good, didn't I?"

Chuckling, Sam ruffled Craig's hair. "Yeah, you did good."

"What'd I tell you?" Craig said to Leah. "And if I can handle Sam's big truck, the Mustang oughta be a piece of cake."

"We'll see," she said vaguely.

The familiar beep-beep of Patrice's car horn sounded from outside. "There's your mom," she said to Craig. "Hurry and get your things."

Craig scooped his backpack from the kitchen table and raced for the door. "Wait till I tell her I drove Sam's truck. She's gonna flip out for sure!"

The back door slammed behind Craig, leaving Leah and Sam alone in the kitchen.

Though Leah wanted to put her head down and

weep at the thought of Sam leaving, she pasted on a cheerful smile. "Well, you certainly made his day."

Sam lifted a shoulder. "He deserved a treat for cutting off that mop of hair."

"Were you behind that, too?"

He shrugged again. "I might've planted the seed."

"You've been a tremendous influence on him. I don't know how to thank you for all you've done."

"No thanks needed. He's a good kid."

Afraid if she didn't do something she would drop to her knees and beg him to stay, she opened the dishwasher door and began unloading the clean dishes. "Did you see his face when he left? I haven't seen him that excited or happy in ages."

"Doesn't take much to make a kid happy."

She stretched to place a stack of plates in the cupboard. "He used to be such a happy guy. Laughing all the time. I'd forgotten what it was like to see him smile."

"Leah—"

Something in his voice told her she didn't want to hear what he had to say, and she cut him off. "I can't believe you're almost finished with the Mustang."

"Still needs to be painted. You'll have to find someone local to do that for you. Leah, I need to—"

She closed the dishwasher door and turned for the refrigerator. "I'll bet your hungry. I know I am. I think there's some salad left from last night. I could toss in some grilled chicken and maybe some feta cheese—"

He caught her arm and turned her around, forcing her to meet his gaze. "Leah," he said firmly. "We need to talk."

His expression was so somber, his tone so serious, she wanted to clap her hands over her ears to keep from hearing whatever it was he wanted to say.

Instead she sat down at the table. "If it's about you leaving…" she began, hoping that broaching the subject herself would take some of the sting out of him saying it.

He shook his head and took the seat opposite hers. "No. It isn't that."

She looked at him in puzzlement. "Is something wrong?"

"Would you do me a favor?" He stretched out a hand. "Would you hold my hand?"

She laughed nervously. "Sam, you're scaring me. What's this all about?"

"Just hold my hand. Please."

Gulping, she placed her hand over his palm.

He curved his fingers around hers, gripped them tightly. "I haven't been totally honest with you."

Stunned, she tried to pull her hand free, but he tightened his grip, refusing to let her go.

"Please, hear me out."

She jutted her chin, knowing she had no other choice. "All right."

"I'm not a mechanic."

She stared, then laughed. "Don't be ridiculous. Of course you're a mechanic! I've seen you work on the car."

"You don't have to be a mechanic to know how to fix a car."

Her smile slowly faded and she searched his face, waiting for him to laugh, to tell her he was pulling her leg, that this was all some huge joke. But his expression remained somber, his blue eyes steady on hers.

"But…why?" she asked. "Why would you lie?"

He lowered his gaze and stroked a thumb across the back of her hand. "Because I knew you'd send me packing if you knew who I really am."

Her eyes widened in alarm. "You're not Sam Forrester?"

His lips curved in a wan smile. "Sam I am. It's the rest I kept from you."

Her mind whirled with questions, a thousand possibilities, but she couldn't bring herself to voice a single one.

"If you'll remember, I told you I had taken a sabbatical, to consider a career change."

"Is that what this is about?" she asked hopefully. "You've decided what you want to do?"

He shook his head. "To be honest, I've been so caught up in your life I haven't given much thought to my own."

Guilt stabbed at her. "I'm sorry. I didn't mean to drag you into my family's problems."

"I'm not sorry. In fact, I've enjoyed being here with you. Getting to know you and Craig. The thing is, Leah, I don't want to leave."

Her eyes widened in surprise.

He grasped her hand between both of his. "I told you I was from Lampasas, and that's true…to an extent. Lampasas is where I grew up, but I don't have a home there." He snorted a wry breath. "Hell, I don't have a home at all, which is one of the reasons I took the sabbatical."

His expression softened and he gave her hand a squeeze.

"Then I met you. I know we haven't known each other all that long, but I've grown to…care for you and I'd like the chance to play that out, see where it leads."

Leah swallowed hard, unsure how much of her own feelings to reveal. "I'd like that, too."

He lowered his gaze to their joined hands, tapped his thumb against hers. "There's just one problem. More than one, really."

"If it's because I'm so obsessive about every-thing—" she said quickly, fearing that was the reason behind his reluctance to make a commitment.

He shook his head. "No. I can live with your anal-yzing." He lifted his head and met her gaze. "I've looked death in the face more times than I care to think about, but I've never been as scared as I am right now."

Aware of the tremble in his hands, the uncertainty that shadowed his eyes, she didn't doubt for a second that what he said was true. "I don't understand. What is there to be scared of?"

"Losing you."

"Oh, Sam," she said, her heart melting. "Why would you think you could lose me?"

"Because I'm a soldier."

She froze, praying that she had misunderstood. "Did you say…soldier?"

At his nod, she shot to her feet, this time succeeding in pulling her hand from his. "No," she said, backing away. "No. No. No."

He stood and reached for her. "Leah."

She jerked away. "No! I won't go through this again. I can't."

"Leah, please."

"No!" she cried. "I lost my father and brother. I won't go through that again. I can't. The waiting, the worrying. Fearing that every time the doorbell rings it's a chaplain coming to deliver bad news." She shook her head. "I can't do that. I won't. Not even for you."

Sam stuffed his spare boots into the duffel, zipped the bag closed, then reared back and hurled the duffel against the door. He was mad. Good and damn mad. And, as the old saying went, he was getting the hell out of Dodge.

He'd known going in what Leah's reaction would be when he told her what he did for a living…but knowing how she'd react and living the experience were two entirely different matters.

She had hurt him, dammit. For the first time in his life he'd offered a woman his heart, and she'd drop-kicked it back into his face.

And all because he was a soldier, a man who loved his country, was willing to fight for it, lay down his life in the name of freedom.

Well, to hell with her, he told himself as he stormed to the bathroom to collect his shaving kit. If she wanted to live the rest of her days in fear of what *might* happen, so be it. He wasn't going to sit around crying in his beer over a woman who'd allow a tragic past to twist her up so much emotionally she was afraid to live.

To hell with her, he thought again. There were other fish in the sea. Leah Kittrell wasn't the only single woman left in the world.

Groaning, he sagged down on the bed and dropped his face to his hands. Who was he trying to kid? he asked himself miserably. She may not be the only woman left in the world, but she was the only one who mattered to him.

With a sigh, he dragged his hands down his face and braced his arms on his thighs, trying to think what to do. Attempting to talk to her again would be a waste of time. No amount of reasoning was going to change her feelings about the military. She'd spent too many years building her wall of resentment for him to have a hope of knocking it down in the time he had left.

Four days and he had to report back to headquarters. And he had only a day, two at the most, of work left to do on the car. Not enough time to undo all the damage losing her family had done to her.

But he could keep his end of their agreement, he told himself. He'd finish the car, thus fulfilling her brother's promise to Craig.

Rising, he crossed to his duffel and picked it up.

But in return, Leah was going to help him fulfill a promise.

The one he'd made to Mack.

The sun was barely up when Sam lifted the hood of the Mustang and began work on the engine. He'd been at it for nearly two hours when he heard the kitchen door open and knew it was Leah leaving for work.

He'd thought she would ignore him, climb into her SUV and drive away without acknowledging his presence.

Instead she marched straight toward him.

"You don't need to concern yourself with the car

any longer," she said coolly. "I'll find someone else to finish the job."

If she'd slapped him, she couldn't have hurt him any more.

He straightened to face her. "You said you wanted to fulfill your brother's promise to restore the Mustang for Craig and hired me for the job. I finish what I start. And I intend to see that your brother's promise is met."

She opened her mouth, then closed it with a click of teeth and spun away.

Sam grabbed her arm and spun her back around. "You never asked me why I came here."

She snatched free, her eyes snapping with anger. "And listen to another lie? Sorry. I've heard all the lies I want to hear from you."

He bit down on his temper, determined to tell her whether she wanted to hear it or not. "I came at the request of a friend. His wife's father served with yours in Vietnam."

She jerked up her chin. "I don't care why you came. Your leaving is all that interests me."

"Then I can put your mind at rest. I'll be pulling out as soon as I finish the car. But I'm taking something with me, when I go."

She eyed him suspiciously. "W-what?"

"I promised Mack I'd get the information he wanted. His wife has a torn piece of paper her father sent her mother while he was in Vietnam. Addy thinks your father might have sent your mother a similar piece."

She sucked in a shocked breath at the mention of Addy's name. "Addy McGruder?"

"Yeah, the lady you refused to talk to on the phone, the one whose letters you never answered. Unlike you, she cares about her father and wants to resolve the mystery surrounding his life."

She flinched at the accusation, then jutted her chin. "I was two years old when my father was in Vietnam, too young to read whatever letters he sent my mother."

"That may be, but your mother read them. Probably kept them, too. Addy says the pieces of paper, when combined, might have some value. She doesn't care about the money. She only wants to add another piece to the puzzle in hopes of discovering what it was her father went to such lengths to see that she received."

She hesitated a moment, and he was sure that she was going to agree to give him the information he needed.

Instead she turned for her car.

"Tell your friend I'm sorry," she called over her shoulder, "but I can't help her."

He swore under his breath at her stubbornness, then shouted, "Can't or won't?"

She stumbled a step, then squared her shoulders and strode on.

* * *

Sam's cell phone rang. Since his hands were full, pouring oil into the crankcase, he said to Craig, "Get that, would you?"

"Sure."

Craig plucked the cell phone from the holder at Sam's waist and punched the connect button. "Sam's personal secretary," he wisecracked.

Chuckling, Sam shook his head while Craig listened to the caller's response.

Craig snatched the phone from his ear and shoved it at Sam. "It's some mean-sounding dude," he whispered. "Says it's a matter of national security."

Sam dropped the oil stick and swore when it dropped down into the engine.

"I'll get it," Craig offered and bumped the phone against Sam's arm. "You better see what he wants."

Mindful of the oil that slicked his hands, Sam gingerly lifted the phone to hold between his shoulder and ear while he pulled a rag from his back pocket. "Forrester," he said curtly, then chuckled when he recognized Jack's voice.

"Your timing sucks," he said to his friend. "I'm hip-deep in a Mustang's engine."

He listened a moment, then caught the phone and held it closer to his ear, his amusement fading. "Say that again."

He listened intently while Jack repeated his findings. "Are they sending in a team?" he asked.

"What do you mean, 'That's the good part'?" he said, in response to Jack's reply.

He sank weakly against the Mustang, bracing his hips against the grill. "Yeah," he said drily after Jack explained. "That's ironic, all right. Guess I better call headquarters and find out when I'm scheduled to leave."

"Yeah, me, too," he said to Jack's wish that he could go along for the ride. "But desk jockeys aren't allowed in the field, remember?"

Smiling, he nodded. "Yeah, yeah. I've heard that story before."

He listened again, then shook his head. "No, I haven't made a decision yet." He glanced down as Craig scooted from beneath the Mustang, the oil stick in hand. Noticing the stricken look on the boy's face, he said to Jack, "Listen. I gotta go. Appreciate your help, buddy. Next time I'm in D.C. I'll buy you a beer."

He disconnected the call and pushed the phone back into the holster at his waist, then extended a hand and pulled Craig to his feet.

His eyes fixed on Sam's, Craig asked hesitantly, "You're leaving?"

Sam dropped his chin to his chest. "Yeah. Looks that way."

"But what about the car? You haven't got it running yet."

Sam heard the panic in the kid's voice and knew

it was more than the car he was worried about. He slung an arm around the boy's shoulder. "It will be by morning. You can bank on that."

Sam figured it was an indication of a masochistic side of his personality he wasn't aware of, but he felt it only right that he should let Leah know that he was leaving in the morning.

Since he no longer considered it appropriate to use the key she had given him, he knocked on the kitchen door, then waited for her response.

He didn't have to wait long.

"What do you want?" she asked curtly through the small crack she'd made in the opening.

He stuck his hands in his pockets to keep himself from shoving the door wide and shaking some sense into her. "Just wanted to let you know I'll be leaving in the morning. I'll strip the bed and do the laundry before I go. The keys to the apartment and the house will be on the kitchen table."

There was a long stretch of silence in which Sam held his breath, silently praying that it was a sign that she regretted the things she'd said, might even be about to beg him to stay.

His hopes were dashed when she said, "Fine," and closed the door in his face.

Leah knelt before her bedroom window, her gaze on the canopy below. Sam had hung lights on each of the poles supporting the covering, directing their beams on the Mustang. Though it was dark, the lights gave Leah a clear view of the canopy and the immediate area around it. But the canopy's canvas blocked her view of Sam.

She glanced at the illuminated dial of her wristwatch and saw that it was three in the morning. She turned her gaze back to the window, unable to believe he was still outside working. She supposed when he'd told her he finished what he started, that, at least, hadn't been a lie.

She felt the swell of tears and bit her lip, willing them back. A soldier, she thought, balling her hand into a fist against the sill. Of all the men in the world to choose from, why did she have to fall in love with a soldier?

She heard the whine of an engine cranking and held her breath, waiting for it to catch. The sound stopped, started again. Stopped, started again. When it caught, the powerful roar of the engine filled the night, then settled to a low hum.

She smiled through her tears, remembering that sound and the long nights Kevin had spent as a teenager doing exactly what Sam was doing now. Revving the engine, letting it idle to listen to the purr, revving it again. *Boys and their toys,* she had teased Kevin.

But Kevin had been determined to make the car

run again. It was if he'd believed that in doing so he could bring their father back to life, too.

Sighing, she propped her chin on her arms on the windowsill. Their mother wasn't the only one who'd never given up hope on their father returning home. That same hope had burned in Kevin, too.

Seven

When Leah returned home from work, her gaze settled on the two keys sitting on the center of the table. He was gone. Sam had really left her.

Feeling the swell of tears, she set her jaw and turned away, dropping her briefcase over the top of the keys to block them from sight. "Craig?" she called. "Where are you?"

"In here," he yelled.

Prepared to deliver a lecture if he was watching television without having completed his homework assignments, she strode to the den.

She found him sitting on the floor in front of the

bookcases. "What are you doing?" she asked in puzzlement as she squatted down beside him.

He lifted an opened book from his lap. Her
stomach knotted when she saw that he was holding
the family photo album.

"Look at this," he said and plopped the book on
his lap again to point. "It's a picture of Dad standing
beside the Mustang."

She gulped but eased closer. She remembered
when the picture was taken. It was the day Kevin
had registered the Mustang and received the new set
of license plates making the vehicle legal to drive.
He'd spent months working on the car, putting it
back in running condition and doing the repairs
required to pass state inspection. His pride was
obvious in the swell of his chest, the smile on his
face. He'd been seventeen at the time and obsessed
by the memory of a father he'd never known.

She sank down beside Craig and draped an arm
along his shoulders. "You look like him," she said
softly.

He turned his head to peer at her. "You think so?"

Smiling, she brushed back his much shorter
bangs from his forehead. "Yes, I do. Sometimes
when I look at you, it's like seeing him at your age."

A slow smile spread across his face. "Really?
Cool." He dropped his gaze to study the picture
again. "See that?" he asked, pointing to a dent on the
Mustang's rear panel. "That's not there anymore.

Sam took it out. Used this giant suction cup. Said if it had been any deeper, a body shop would've had to do the work because it would require filling and sanding."

She gulped back emotion at the mention of Sam. "Yes, I would imagine it would."

He turned to peer at her. "He's gone, you know."

She swallowed hard. "Yeah, I know."

"He left me a note."

Pain pierced her heart at the thoughtfulness in the gesture. She wanted to ask what Sam had written in the note, if he had mentioned her, but said instead, "That's nice."

"He's going to Vietnam."

Stunned, for a moment she could only stare. "How do you know where he is going?"

"Sam told me. And get this—he's on a secret mission to recover MIAs."

She closed her eyes, afraid if she didn't she would shatter into a thousand pieces.

"He's hoping he'll find my grandfather."

She flipped open her eyes. "Your grandfather is *dead*," she said furiously.

He drew back, with a frown. "I know that. But his body was never found. That's why he doesn't have a grave like Grandma's."

She surged to her feet. "He doesn't have a grave because your grandmother refused to accept the fact that he was dead!"

"Why are you yelling at me?" he shouted back at her. "I didn't do anything."

She dug her fingernails into her palms, fighting for calm, knowing Craig didn't deserve her anger. "I'm sorry. I didn't mean to yell."

Scowling, he slammed the book shut and shoved it back onto the shelf. "Sam was right," he grumbled as he pushed to his feet.

When he would've brushed past her, she caught his arm, stopping him. "Right about what?"

He snatched his arm free. "You're mad at everybody for dying. My dad, your dad, Grandma. You're mad at 'em all."

Leah couldn't sleep that night. She kept thinking about what Craig had said.

You're mad at everybody for dying. My dad, your dad, Grandma. You're mad at 'em all.

She wanted to deny his statement. In fact, she had spent the last six hours attempting to do just that, if only to convince herself.

But she couldn't deny it any longer. She *was* mad. At her father, her mother, her brother. Each of their deaths—in her mind, at least—had been senseless, avoidable. If her father hadn't joined the Army, he wouldn't have been killed. If her mother had accepted her father's death, she never would have committed suicide. And if her mother had focused on meeting Kevin's needs rather than infecting her son with her own obsession, Kevin wouldn't have joined the Army and been killed in Iraq.

Whether their deaths had been avoidable or not, they were gone, and being angry with them for dying wasn't going to bring them back. She knew that...or at least she did intellectually. It was her heart she couldn't convince.

She heaved a sigh, thinking of all the years she had spent resenting her mother for clinging to the hope that her husband would come home someday. She had considered her mother's obsession foolish, misguided, an emotional sickness that kept her, as well as the rest of their family, from living a normal life.

In retrospect, Leah could see that her anger wasn't all that different from her mother's obsession. By clinging to it, she had allowed it to control her life, her actions...and, it seemed, destroy her future.

She turned her face to the pillow, ashamed of the way she'd treated Sam. She'd said such horrible things to him, insulted his choice of career, something he obviously felt strongly about. Worse, she had let him leave without telling him she cared for him, too, that, like him, she wanted a chance to let their relationship play out, see where it took them.

And all because he was a soldier.

With a groan, she rolled to her back and pressed the heels of her hands against her eyes as her mind circled back to the source of the problem: Sam's chosen career.

It didn't matter how much she cared for him. She couldn't live the life of a soldier's wife. The fear, the worry, the loneliness. She hated the military. It was the military that had destroyed her family, cutting huge chunks out of her heart, her life.

No, she'd been right in letting Sam leave without sharing her feelings with him or asking him to stay. If she had, she would've only been postponing the inevitable. She could never become seriously involved with a soldier and she certainly could never marry one. How could she when she knew that would mean living her life in fear of having what was left of her heart ripped from her chest?

She rolled from the bed. But she could do something for him, she told herself as she tugged on her robe. She could return at least a part of the kindness he'd shown her. She could help him keep his promise to Mack.

She didn't know if the piece of paper he'd mentioned existed, but she knew where to look.

Leah stood in the doorway of the attic, staring at the tower of mismatched boxes that lined one wall. The sight alone was enough to make her skin crawl, as they represented her mother's obsession. Crammed inside the boxes was every document, report or newspaper clipping printed about the

POWs and MIAs from the Vietnam war. Pictures and souvenirs her father had sent home. The hundreds of letters he'd written to her mother.

After her mother's death, she'd intended to throw the entire mess away, had even carried one load to the curb for the garbage service to pick up. But when she'd returned with the second, she'd discovered she couldn't do it, couldn't throw her mother's dreams away. So she'd loaded up the boxes and brought them to her home to store in her attic.

And there they'd remained, undisturbed for the past six years.

She had never opened the boxes, never had a desire to explore their contents. She knew what was inside. Throughout her life she had watched her mother build her stash, filling box after box with her dreams, her hopes. Sometimes she'd find her mother sifting through the contents, tears streaming down her face; at others she'd be digging through them with a frenetic frenzy, as if the key to locating her husband was buried inside and she had only to find it.

Taking a bracing breath, Leah forced herself to approach the wall of boxes and scanned the scrawled words on their fronts until she found the one marked *Letters*. She carried the box to the center of the room and knelt down, placing it on the floor in front of her and folding back the flaps.

She balled her hand into a fist to still her fingers'

trembling, then reached inside and pulled out a handful of envelopes. Giving in to her need for order, she sat down and, using her lap for a desk, began to sort them by the postal dates stamped on the front. She tensed when her own name seemed to leap at her from the front of an envelope. Unlike the other letters, where the addresses were written in cursive, this one was penned in a first-grader's print, each letter standing alone. She blinked back tears, knowing that he'd written it that way especially for her.

Anxious to read what he'd written, she dashed the tears away and pulled out the single page tucked inside.

Hi, pumpkin!
How's my little girl doing today? Daddy sure misses you. I hope you're taking good care of Mommy. I really liked the picture you drew of her. Her belly is really getting big! I'll bet you grow up to be an artist someday.

Mommy tells me you don't want a little sister, only a little brother. Well, I hate to tell you this, pumpkin, but you don't get to choose. God decides whether our baby will be a boy or a girl. Since He knows best, we'll love whatever He sends us. Right?

Every night before I go to sleep I pull out the picture of you and Mommy I carry in my

*pocket and tell you good night. Do you hear
me when I say it? I hear you saying it back to
me. And when I put the picture against my
cheek I can feel your sweet good-night kisses.*

*I bet you've grown a foot since I saw you
last. Tell Mommy to put a rock on your head
so that you won't grow any more, okay?*

*You be a good girl and take care of Mommy
for me. I miss you, baby, and I can't wait to
see you again.*

Love,
Daddy

Choked by tears, Leah stared at the words he'd
written, sensing his loneliness, overwhelmed by the
love that all but poured from the page. Pressing the
letter against her heart, she closed her eyes, trying
to draw an image of him in her mind. She had no
memories to pull from, only the photographs her
mother had kept scattered around their home. She
was too young to recall the things he'd mentioned
in the letter—kissing him good-night, him calling
her "pumpkin." But it was obvious that he'd remembered and had treasured those memories while he'd
been away, in order to keep her close to his heart.

Guilt seized her, a shame that sliced to the marrow
of her bones. He'd clung to her memory while she'd
done everything humanly possible to block his.

Not any longer, she told herself and scooped up

the letters, stuffed them back into the box. Lifting it, she stood and stumbled her way downstairs, then returned for the box of pictures and souvenirs.

Her movements were frantic as she pulled item after item from the boxes, determined to get to know the man she'd spent a lifetime shunning.

"Aunt Leah?"

She jumped at the sound of Craig's voice, then called, "In here!" and went back to her sorting.

"Are you sick or something?"

She glanced up and saw the concern in his eyes. "No, sweetheart. I'm fine. Why?"

"It's almost noon and you've still got on your pajamas."

She looked down and sputtered a laugh, not realizing until that moment that she'd never bothered to get dressed. From the moment she'd hauled the last box to her den she had thought of nothing else but the box's contents.

She cleared a spot on the carpet. "Come and help me."

He dropped down beside her. "What are you doing?"

"Getting to know my father."

He looked at her warily. "Are you sure you're not sick?"

Laughing, she gave him a hug. "No. I'm perfectly fine. In fact, I've never felt better."

"If you say so," he said doubtfully.

She picked up a pile of letters and dumped them in his lap. "We're on a treasure hunt," she told him and picked up another stack for herself to examine.

"Treasure?"

"Yes. A torn piece of paper. I don't know what it looks like or what it is exactly, but I know it's got to be here somewhere."

"A torn piece of paper," he repeated doubtfully.

"Yes. Sam told me about it. That's why he came here. To find it."

He picked up an envelope from those scattered on his lap. "Is the piece of paper a clue or something he needs to find the MIAs in Vietnam?"

Busy shaking the pages of the letter she held, she shook her head. "No. This is something that my dad sent home to my mother while he was in Vietnam. Sam says it may be valuable."

"Is that why he wants it? Because it's worth money?"

She tossed aside the letter and picked up another. "No. It's actually a friend of his who wants it. Or rather, his friend's wife. Her father served in the same unit as my dad. She has a piece of paper, too. It's like a puzzle we have to put together."

"Cool!"

Obviously excited at the prospect of finding treasure, he shook out the envelope's contents, examined the pages, tossed them aside, grabbed another.

Leah picked up a letter but frowned when she noticed that the handwriting on the front was different from the others. Curious, she pulled out the letter enclosed and began to scan. She'd read only two lines when she flung out a hand and grabbed Craig's arm. "Listen to this," she said in disbelief, then read,

"Dear Helen,
We've never met, but I would imagine your husband has mentioned me a time or two. My name is Larry Blair—or Pops, as the guys in our unit call me. T.J. made me promise that I'd write to you if anything should happen to him. It grieves me that I have to keep that promise now, but I can't let T.J. down. I gave him my word.

The day before T.J. was shot, we lost a guy in our unit. Buddy Crandall. We were caught in a battle we couldn't win and had decided to make a run for it. Several of our men went down prior to the decision being made. We managed to drag two of them out with us, but we couldn't get to Buddy. We knew he was dead and there was nothing we could do for him, but it broke our hearts to leave a friend behind. T.J. took it particularly hard.

The next morning, when the chopper came

to retrieve the bodies, T.J.'s thoughts were on Buddy's family. He knew, we all did, that since Buddy's body wasn't recovered, he would be listed as Missing in Action rather than as Killed in Action. That bothered T.J., as he was worried about Buddy's family and how not having him to bury would affect them. It was then that T.J. made me promise to write this letter should the same thing happen to him.

I saw T.J. go down. You don't need to know the details of how he died. I can spare you that much pain. But please know that he fought bravely to the bitter end. And know, too, that if it had been within our power, we would have brought T.J. back with us. He'd have done the same for any one of the rest of us, and we would've done it for him if it had been possible. No soldier ever wants to leave a friend on the field.

Along with this letter, I send you my heart-felt sympathy, as well as that of the rest of our unit. T.J. was a good man, a good friend and was never shy about telling us how much he loved his family.

Sincerely,
Larry Blair"

Leah sat in silence, staring down at the handwritten words, unable to believe her mother had continued to hope her husband would come after having read Larry Blair's letter.

"I don't get it."

Having forgotten about Craig, Leah reached to squeeze his hand. "What, sweetheart?"

"Why would Grandma keep telling everybody he was going to come home when the letter proves he was dead?"

She gulped back tears and shook her head. "Hope. She loved him too much to give up believing he'd come home someday."

"That's just stupid," Craig muttered and picked up another envelope to examine.

They worked together for almost an hour before Craig let out a whoop.

"I found it!" he cried.

Leah dropped the letter she was reading and stared. "Are you sure?"

"It has to be." He examined the piece of paper closely. "There's words on it, but they don't make any sense."

He pushed the paper at Leah. "See if you can figure it out."

Afraid it would crumble if handled overmuch, Leah laid the scrap of paper on the floor in front of her. "Doesn't make sense to me either," she murmured as she studied the partial words fragmented by the tears. Frowning, she turned the piece of paper over. "But that's my father's signature."

She popped to her feet. "Call your mother. Tell her that you're going on a little trip with me."

He jumped up, too, to run after her. "Where are we going?"

"To fulfill a promise Sam made to his friend."

Leah smiled as she watched Craig play with the baby. Stretched out on his stomach on the floor, he lay head-to-head with the infant, spinning dials and punching buttons on a learning toy to make the baby laugh.

"Careful, Craig," she warned as he tried to persuade the baby to push one of the buttons. "Remember, he's just a baby."

She started to rise to intervene, and Mack placed a hand on her arm, stopping her. "Leave 'em be. They're doing fine."

"Are you sure?" she asked doubtfully. "Craig's never been around a baby before."

"They aren't as fragile as they look."

A shrill squeal had Leah whipping her head back to the two, her heart in her throat.

Mack chuckled. "That's Johnny Mack's newest form of expression. Means he's having a good time."

Leah sank back weakly against the sofa. "If you say so."

"Craig's good with babies. Most boys his age would be bored to death by now."

She smiled sadly as she watched Craig dab a cloth at the drool on the infant's chin. "He always wanted a brother or sister."

"Sam told me about your brother. I'm sorry for your loss."

Her heart twisted at the mention of Sam, then twisted again at the thought of Kevin. "Thank you. Losing him was hard on us all. Especially Craig."

Mack turned his gaze to study Craig. "He seems to be doing okay. Kids are tough. Resilient. He'll come out of this okay."

She glanced his way. "You sound so sure."

He smiled and patted her knee. "The voice of experience."

She stared, remembering the stories Sam had told her about his wild friend and the half brother who was responsible for turning Sam's life around. "You're Ty's half brother?"

He lifted a brow. "You know Ty?"

She shook her head. "No. Sam told me about him. How you were always bailing the two of them out of trouble."

"Still am. Or was," he amended.

Understanding the defeat she heard in his voice, she laid a hand over his. "You may have failed with Ty, but you certainly made an impression on Sam. He credits you with saving his life."

He smiled fondly. "Sam was a good kid. A little wild, but he had a good heart. His parents are to blame for the problems he had. They were so busy fighting they forgot they had a son to raise."

Leah glanced at Craig, knowing that her nephew suffered similarly. His mother was so consumed with her own grief she never recognized that her son was grieving, too, and needed her comfort. As a result, he'd looked for attention elsewhere and found it with a group of thugs.

But she'd seen a change in him recently, she reminded herself. He laughed more, showed more enthusiasm for life, stayed closer to home rather than hanging out with his friends. "Thanks to Sam," she murmured, knowing it was Sam who was responsible for the difference.

"Excuse me?"

She glanced at Mack and dropped her gaze, embarrassed that she'd spoken her thoughts out loud. "Sorry. I was thinking about Sam, the difference he's made in Craig's life." She looked up at Mack. "It's because of you. What you did for Sam, Sam did for Craig."

"What goes around, comes around," Mack stated prophetically, then smiled. "Sam was always hanging around our house. He was like a brother to me. I worried about him." He shook his head sadly. "In fact, I still do."

Her stomach knotted, remembering where Sam was, what he was doing. The danger he might be in. "I wish he hadn't gone."

He gave her knee a reassuring pat. "He'll be all right. Sam knows how to take care of himself." He shook his head. "But I wasn't talking about his profession. Sam's struggling with a decision right now. Trying to decide whether to take a desk job or remain in the field. It's a tough one for a man like him to make. He's not one to sit on his hands. When he sees a problem, he'd rather be in on the action to resolve it than sitting in a meeting discussing it."

"Then why is he considering changing?" Leah asked in confusion.

"Sam could probably explain that best." He opened his hands. "I've never had any military experience, so I don't know that I completely understand it myself. But from what Sam has told me, it seems if a man remains in the field too long, he begins to lose his edge, take unnecessary chances. It becomes a game to him, one in which he's constantly raising the stakes in order to achieve the same adrenalin high."

Leah stared, wondering if that was why Kevin had volunteered for duty in Iraq. He'd enlisted in the service shortly after his eighteenth birthday and had remained in the Army until his death. His assignments had taken him all over the world. Korea. The Philippines. Japan.

Had he grown bored? she wondered. Was that why he'd requested a tour in Iraq? Was it the danger he'd sought and not the need to prove something, as she'd always believed?

She gulped, unsure of the answer.

"But I think there's more bothering Sam than just a career decision," Mack went on to say. "I believe he's questioning his life right now. His lack of roots. Lack of family. He's thirty-four years old, an age when most men have settled down with a wife, a home and one-point-five children.

"He's had an exciting life, traveled the world. But I think he's beginning to realize there's something missing, something only a family can provide."

He tipped his head to peer down at Leah. "I thought he'd found that with you. From the things he told me, I was sure that he'd finally found the woman who made him want to settle down, quit thumbing his nose at danger. Was I wrong?"

She dropped her gaze. "I care for Sam. I do. But I'm not cut out to be a soldier's wife. I couldn't stand living with the fear that he might not come home someday. I've lost two people I love to the service. I won't lose any more."

"Where did they go?"

She looked up at him in confusion. "My father and brother?"

"No, your feelings for Sam. Did he take them with him when he left? Did you flush them down the toilet? Throw them in the trash?"

She drew back with a frown, wondering if he'd lost his mind. "Of course not. I still care for him."

"Then what does it matter if he's with you or halfway around the world? If you love him, you'll feel the loss either way."

Eight

After completing his ten-day mission in Vietnam, Sam flew directly to Washington, D.C., where he was to meet with his commander and file his report. If he'd had his way, the plane would've flown directly to Texas. Specifically Tyler, Texas. The pilot wouldn't even have had to worry about landing. Sam would've jumped to save himself the time a landing would've required.

Soon enough, he promised himself and forced himself to concentrate on the report he was giving.

"Four bodies recovered, possibly more," he told his commander. "The lab guys can verify the number and provide names, depending on the availability of dental records and possibly DNA."

"So our contact was correct in telling us we'd find bodies in that location."

"Yes, sir," Sam confirmed. He folded his beret and laid it across his thigh. "The local officials were cooperative. Not helpful," he clarified. "But they didn't attempt to obstruct our examination of the area in question."

The commander nodded solemnly. "The best we can expect under the circumstances." He frowned, considering. "Any chance more bodies were buried there?"

"In that particular location?"

The commander nodded.

"I suppose it's possible, but our search was methodic and the equipment we used was the best technology has to offer. I don't see how we could've missed finding anything more than what we brought home."

The commander gave his chin a decisive nod. "Your opinion is good enough for me. Your record speaks for itself. You're thorough and have the reputation of sticking with a task to its end. Which brings up another subject." Rearing back in his chair, the commander templed his fingers before his chest and studied Sam over their tips. "Your reenlistment. Have you made your decision concerning your assignment?"

"Yes, sir, I have."

When Sam offered nothing more, the commander said impatiently, "Well? Do you plan to share your decision or keep it to yourself?"

"I've put in sixteen years, sir, and I think it's time I returned to civilian life."

"I'm sorry to hear that," the commander said with regret. "Our country needs good men like you."

"Thank you, sir. I've enjoyed my time in the service, and I'm grateful for the knowledge and experience I've gained. Hopefully I'll be able to find a way to continue to serve my country as a civilian."

"I'm sure you will. If I can be of assistance in helping you find your calling, let me know."

"Thank you, sir."

The commander stood, signaling the end of the meeting. "So where are you headed now?"

Sam stood, too. "Home, sir. To Texas." He hesitated a moment, knowing the favor he was about to ask broke protocol and probably every other military regulation.

"Something on your mind, Forrester?" the commander asked.

Sam nodded slowly. "Yes, sir, there is. One of the sets of dog tags found belonged to the father of a friend of mine. I'd appreciate it if you would allow me to personally deliver them to her and give her the news that her father's body was recovered."

The commander squared his shoulders. "You

know as well as I do that information is considered classified until the bodies have been positively ID'd."

"Yes, sir, I do. But this family's suffering exceeds those normally associated with an MIA. They need closure, and I would like to be the one to give it to them."

"I'm sorry, Forrester, but I can't allow that. Everything that was collected during the exhumation was shipped directly to the lab for identification."

Sam ducked his head. "Uh, not everything, sir. I have the dog tags that were collected. Each set was bagged on-site and properly marked with location and placed in my pack for safekeeping."

"Your orders were to collect all items found during the exhumation and escort them home in the container provided."

Sam felt a trickle of sweat work its way down his spine, knowing what he'd done had defied a direct order and could result in a reprimand…or worse, if the commander chose to pursue it.

"Yes, sir. I'm aware of that. But considering the sensitive nature of our findings and the hostility that still surrounds our presence in some areas of Vietnam, I thought it best to keep the tags on my person."

Scowling, the commander rounded his desk and walked with Sam to the door. "Those tags are the property of the United States Army and fall under its jurisdiction. I order you to turn them over to proper authorities ASAP."

All hope of presenting Leah with the closure she needed drained from Sam. "Yes, sir. I'll take care of it as soon I leave this office."

The commander stopped at the doorway and shot Sam a sideways glance. "You said four bodies were found?"

"As best as we could determine. Possibly more."

"And how many sets of tags were recovered?"

"Three."

"Were the tags positioned in such a way that you were able to determine which body each belonged to?"

"Yes, sir. Without question. We digitally recorded each find before moving so much as a grain of sand."

"So if a set of tags were to disappear or become lost, it wouldn't effect the results of your mission or lessen the chances of identifying the bodies?"

A smile began to spread across Sam's face as he realized what the commander was trying to tell him. "No, sir. Not at all."

Leah had thought she would feel better after giving a copy of the torn piece of paper to Addy McGruder—Mack's wife—thus fulfilling Sam's promise to his friend…as well as the request he'd made of Leah. But, if anything, her trip to Lampasas had left her feeling more miserable and confused than ever.

It wasn't that she hadn't liked Sam's friends. She'd enjoyed visiting with the McGruders, and Craig had had a ball playing with their baby, which had been an unexpected bonus for him.

The cause of her discontent was something Mack had said, a question he'd posed while Addy had been preparing their dinner.

Then what does it matter if he's with you or halfway around the world? If you love him, you'll feel the loss either way.

She had wanted to rail at him, tell him that it *did* matter, that he had no right to make such a statement when he'd never suffered as she had.

Thankfully she had bitten her tongue and kept her opinion to herself, which had turned out to be a good thing, as she'd learned later from Addy that Mack had lost his first wife and his son in a car wreck.

Knowing Mack had suffered similarly hadn't diminished her own grief, but it had made her think.

She loved Sam. She didn't doubt her feelings for him for a minute. And she missed him. Oh, God, how she missed him. But as hard as she had tried, she couldn't think of a way for them to be together and both of them be happy.

No closer to a resolution than she had been two weeks earlier, when she'd made the trip to Lampasas, she opened another one of the boxes she'd hauled down from the attic. She'd decided to go through each and every one, catalog its contents and repackage it in something more substantial than the ragged boxes her mother had kept the material in.

She shook her head sadly at her mother's harum-scarum filing system. After days of attempting to find some method to her mother's madness, she'd finally given up and decided to develop her own. She glanced around the room at the reams of paper stacked on every available surface and sputtered a laugh. Of course, she'd destroyed her den in the process. It seemed Leah, the queen of organization, had finally toppled from her thrown.

Hearing the kitchen door open, she picked up a stack of papers and carried them to the pile marked *MIA Reports, 1986–1989,* knowing it was Craig coming to help her.

"In here, Craig," she called, then added, "And bring me a soda, will you? I'm dying of thirst."

She thumbed through the documents, scanning the dates on each, then braced a knee against the stack to support it, while she wedged the papers she held into the proper order.

"Would you settle for a lemonade?"

She whirled, and the stack toppled over, papers sliding to cover the floor. Sam stood less than ten feet away, a glass of lemonade in his hand. Decked out in his dress uniform, he looked handsome, regal…intimidating.

She wanted to tell him she was sorry, that she loved him, but all that came out was a breathy, "Sam."

He held up the glass. "Sorry. No soda. Only lemonade."

She searched his face for any sign of emotion. That he'd missed her. That he loved her. But his expression remained unreadable, his eyes a cool sky-blue.

Gulping, she said, "Lemonade's fine."

He crossed to hand her the glass. She took it and had to grip it between both hands, she was shaking so much.

"When did you—"

"How are—"

They both stopped and he opened a hand. "Ladies first."

"When did you get back?"

"Yesterday." He glanced at his watch. "Or rather, today." At her confused look, he explained. "The time difference. Vietnam's a day ahead of us."

"Oh."

"How are you?"

She forced a smile. "Fine." She glanced around the room. "Busy, as you can tell by the mess."

He crossed to a chair and picked up a document from the stack piled on it. "What's all this?"

"My mother's obsession." When he glanced back at her in question, she shrugged and lifted a hand, indicating all the stacks that filled the room. "These are all the documents, reports and newspapers clippings about MIAs that she saved over the years."

He tossed the document back onto the stack. "What are you doing with it?"

"Sorting, cataloging." She laughed self-consciously. "Being my anal self."

He gave her a chiding look at the anal comment. "I meant, why is it here?"

She drew in a shuddery breath and looked around, thinking of all the discoveries she'd made since opening that first box, how the things she'd found inside had changed her.

"It was all stored in the attic. When I was looking for the piece of paper for Addy, I decided to bring it down and try to put it in some type of order."

"Did you find it?"

"Yes…or rather, Craig did. We took it to her. Craig and I. She was thrilled to have it, but I don't think it was much help."

"You went to Lampasas?" he asked in surprise.

Tears surged and she could only nod.

"But…why? When I asked you to give it to me, you refused. What changed your mind?"

She dropped her gaze and pushed a finger through the condensation on the glass. "I don't know. A lot of things, I guess. Mostly I wanted to do it for you."

"Ah, Leah."

She lifted her head, tears brimming in her eyes. "I'm so sorry, Sam. I know you must hate me for all the awful things I said."

He crossed to take the glass from her and set it aside, so that he could gather her hands in his. He gave them a squeeze. "Not a chance. I couldn't hate you if I tried."

The tears pushed higher. "You were nothing but kind to me, and the one thing you asked of me, I refused."

"It doesn't matter. Not anymore."

She tugged a hand free to drag an arm across her eyes. "I don't know how you can say that after all the mean things I said."

"It's easy to forgive someone you love."

She froze, then slowly lowered her arm to look at him. "You love me?"

Smiling, he nodded. "More than life itself." He reached into his pocket. "I have something for you."

She blinked to clear her eyes and shot them wide when he held up a chain with dog tags dangling at its end. She shifted her gaze to his. "My father's?"

He nodded, then opened her hand and let the chain snake down to pool on her palm. "I found it, along with his remains, outside the village where he was killed." He closed her fingers around the tags. "He's not missing anymore, Leah. Your father's finally coming home."

"Oh, Sam," she said tearfully and threw her arms around his neck. "Thank you. Thank you so much."

He held her tight and pressed his lips against her hair. "I wanted to give you closure, Leah. Your whole family. I just wish your mother could be here to welcome him home and give him the burial he deserves."

She shook her head. "They're together. I know they are. She loved him so much. That's why she took her life. She couldn't stand living without him any longer."

He pushed her to arm's length, his forehead pleated in a frown. "You sound like you've forgiven her, like you're not mad anymore."

She sniffed, shook her head. "Losing my dad destroyed her. Searching for him gave her something to live for. Hope, I guess. She did the best she could for Kevin and me. I realize that now. In her place, I don't know that I could've done any better. Sam—" She stopped and caught his hand, drew him to the sofa, needing its stability beneath her before she told him the rest.

When confronted with the stacks of papers that covered the sofa's cushions, she hesitated a moment, then raked them onto the floor and plopped down.

Sam stared at her in disbelief. "Did I see what I thought I just saw?"

She looked up at him in confusion. "What?"

"Did Leah Kittrell just make a *mess?*"

Pursing her lips, she tugged him down beside her. "Don't be a smart aleck. We need to talk."

"I believe I said those same words before I left for Vietnam."

"Yes, you did. But I wasn't ready to discuss it then. I am now."

He settled back. "Okay. Shoot."

She bit her lower lip, trying to think how best to tell him what she wanted to say. "We love each other," she began carefully.

"I can verify the *W* in that we."

She gave him an exasperated look, then continued. "And when two people love each other, they need to be together."

He draped an arm around her shoulders. "I couldn't agree more."

She drew back, finding it hard to concentrate with him so close. "Your job takes you all over the world, and mine is here in Tyler. I have my family. Responsibilities. I have Craig to think about it. He needs me."

"Yes, he does."

"But I want to be with you."

"And that's a bad thing?"

"No," she said in frustration. "But I can't be with you and here with my family at the same time. I told you that I hated the military, that I couldn't live my life in fear of losing you."

"And that's still true?"

She released a shuddery breath. "Yes. Sort of. But I think I can deal with it better now."

"What brought about the change?"

"Mack."

"Mack?" he repeated.

"Yes. He said something that started me thinking. He said that if I loved you, it wouldn't matter where you were. I'd feel the loss either way."

His smile soft, he swept her hair back from her face. "I always knew that man was a genius."

"You're missing the point," she said, her frustration returning.

"And that would be…?"

"That I love you and want to be with you."

He leaned to press his lips to hers. "Not a problem."

She nearly wept at the feel of his lips on hers but flattened a hand against his chest and pushed him back, refusing to let him distract her until they'd reached an agreement of some kind. "It *is* a problem," she insisted. "I can't be in two places at once."

"You don't have to be."

She filled her hands with her hair. "Sam!" she cried in frustration. "How can we fix this if you won't even admit that we have a problem?"

"Because we don't."

When she glowered at him, he only smiled.

"I resigned from the Army."

For a moment she could only stare. Then she shook her head. "No. I won't let you do that. You love the Army, your job. I won't allow you to sacrifice your happiness for mine."

"Don't you get it? Being here with you, with Craig—that's what important to me. That's what makes me happy." He cupped a hand at her face, holding her gaze to his. "I had a good run, Leah. Sixteen years. But now I want to come home. Start a family. With you, Leah."

She searched his face, afraid to believe what he was telling her, grasp what he was offering her. "Sam, are you sure?"

"As a heart attack."

With a squeal of delight, she threw her arms around his neck and hugged him tight. "Oh, Sam. I want that, too."

She kissed him, holding nothing back, desperate to show him how much she loved him, how much she needed him, what a wonderful life they would have together.

Her heart full to near bursting, she drew back to look at him…and frowned as a thought occurred to her. "But what will you do? For a job, I mean."

He teased her with a smile. "What? Afraid you'll have to support us?"

Pursing her lips, she gave his chest a push. "No. But I know you. You wouldn't be satisfied sitting around doing nothing."

"You're right. I wouldn't. I've been playing with some ideas."

"Like what?"

He pointed a stern finger at her nose. "If I tell you, you have to promise not to go ballistic on me. What I'm considering is perfectly safe."

"I'm not going to go ballistic," she said impatiently. "For heaven's sake, just tell me!"

"I'd like to work with families of POWs and MIAs to help them locate their husbands, sons and brothers."

She pressed her hand over her heart, knowing how much those families needed the closure Sam had given her. "Oh, Sam. That's wonderful."

"I've got skills to offer. Contacts, too. But I wouldn't charge for my services. Only what expenses are incurred. I've set enough back over the years that my savings will take care of our living expenses. We won't be rich by any stretch of the imagination, but we won't starve, either."

"Oh, Sam," she said tearfully. "I don't care about being rich. All I want is for us to be together. Happy. The rest will take care of itself."

He framed her face between his hands. "Marry me, Leah. Nothing would make me happier than having you as my wife, the mother of my children."

Laughing through her tears, she wrapped her arms around him and held him tight. "Yes, yes, a thousand times yes!"

* * * * *

Peggy Moreland's A PIECE OF TEXAS *series
will continue. But don't miss her next release*
MERGER OF FORTUNES, *the first book in
a new continuity, available January 2007
from Silhouette Desire.*

Set in darkness beyond the ordinary world.
Passionate tales of life and death.
With characters' lives ruled by laws the everyday
world can't begin to imagine.

Introducing NOCTURNE, a spine-tingling new
line from Silhouette Books.

The thrills and chills begin with UNFORGIVEN
by Lindsay McKenna

Plucked from the depths of hell, former military sharpshooter Reno Manchahi was hired by the government to kill a thief, but he had a mission of his own. Descended from a family of shape-shifters, Reno vowed to get the revenge he'd thirsted for all these years. But his mission went awry when his target turned out to be a powerful seductress, Magdalena Calen Hernandez, who risked everything to battle a potent evil. Suddenly, Reno had to transform himself into a true hero and fight the enemy that threatened them all. He had to become a Warrior for the Light….

Turn the page for a sneak preview of
UNFORGIVEN by Lindsay McKenna.
On sale September 26, wherever books are sold.

Chapter 1

One shot...one kill.

The sixteen-pound sledgehammer came down with such fierce power that the granite boulder shattered instantly. A spray of glittering mica exploded into the air and sparkled momentarily around the man who wielded the tool as if it were a weapon. Sweat ran in rivulets down Reno Manchahi's drawn, intense face. Naked from the waist up, the hot July sun beating down on his back, he hefted the sledgehammer skyward once more. Muscles in his thick forearms leaped and biceps bulged. Even his breath was focused on the boulder. In his mind's eye, he pictured Army General Robert Hampton's fleshy, arrogant fifty-year-old features on the rock's surface. Air exploded from between his lips as he brought the avenging hammer down. The boulder pulverized beneath his funneled hatred.

One shot...one kill...

Nostrils flaring, he inhaled the dank, humid heat and drew it deep into his massive lungs. Revenge allowed Reno to endure his imprisonment at a U.S. Navy brig near San Diego, California. Drops of sweat were flung in all directions as the crack of his sledgehammer claimed a third stone victim. Mouth taut, Reno moved to the next boulder.

The other prisoners in the stone yard gave him a wide berth. They always did. They instinctively felt his simmering hatred, the palpable revenge in his cinnamon-colored eyes, was more than skin-deep.

And they whispered he was different.

Reno enjoyed being a loner for good reason. He came from a medicine family of shape-shifters. But even this secret power had not protected him—or his family. His wife, Ilona, and his three-year-old daughter, Sarah, were dead. Murdered by Army General Hampton in their former home on USMC base in Camp Pendleton, California. Bitterness thrummed through Reno as he savagely pushed the toe of his scarred leather boot against several smaller pieces of gray granite that were in his way.

The sun beat down upon Manchahi's naked shoulders, grown dark red over time, shouting his half-Apache heritage. With his straight black hair grazing his thick shoulders, copper skin and broad face with high cheekbones, everyone knew he was Indian. When he'd first arrived at the brig, some of the prisoners taunted him and called him Geronimo. Something strange happened to Reno during his fight with the name-calling prisoners. Leaning down after he'd won the scuffle, he'd snarled into each of their bloodied faces that if they were going to call him anything, they would call him *gan,* which was the Apache word for *devil.*

His attackers had been shocked by the wounds on their faces, the deep claw marks. Reno recalled doubling his fist as they'd attacked him en masse. In that split second, he'd gone into an altered state of consciousness. In times of danger, he transformed into a jaguar. A deep, growling sound had emitted from his throat as he defended himself in the three-against-one fracas. It all happened so fast that he thought he had imagined it. He'd seen his hands morph into a forearm and paw, claws extended. The slashes left on the three men's faces after the fight told him he'd begun to shape-shift. A fist made bruises and swelling; not four perfect, deep claw marks. Stunned and anxious, he hid the knowledge of what else he was from these prisoners. Reno's only defense was to make all the prisoners so damned scared of him and remain a loner.

Alone. Yeah, he was alone, all right. The steel

hammer swept downward with hellish ferocity. As the granite groaned in protest, Reno shut his eyes for just a moment. Sweat dripped off his nose and square chin.

Straightening, he wiped his furrowed, wet brow and looked into the pale blue sky. What got his attention was the startling cry of a red-tailed hawk as it flew over the brig yard. Squinting, he watched the bird. Reno could make out the rust-colored tail on the hawk. As a kid growing up on the Apache reservation in Arizona, Reno knew that all animals that appeared before him were messengers.

Brother, what message do you bring me? Reno knew one had to ask in order to receive. Allowing the sledgehammer to drop to his side, he concentrated on the hawk who wheeled in tightening circles above him.

Freedom! the hawk cried in return.

Reno shook his head, his black hair moving against his broad, thickset shoulders. *Freedom? No way, Brother. No way.* Figuring that he was making up the hawk's shrill message, Reno turned away. Back to his rocks. Back to picturing Hampton's smug face.

Freedom!

* * * * *

*Look for UNFORGIVEN by Lindsay McKenna,
the spine-tingling launch title from
Silhouette Nocturne™.*
Available September 26, wherever books are sold.

nocturne™

Save $1.⁰⁰ off

your purchase of any
Silhouette® Nocturne™ novel.

Receive $1.00 off
any Silhouette® Nocturne™ novel.

**Available wherever books are sold, including most
bookstores, supermarkets, drugstores and discount stores.**

Coupon expires December 1, 2006. Redeemable at participating
retail outlets in the U.S. only. Limit one coupon per customer.

5 65373 00076 2   (8100)0 11265

SNCOUPUS

nocturne™

Save $1.⁰⁰ off

your purchase of any
Silhouette® Nocturne™ novel.

Receive $1.00 off

any Silhouette® Nocturne™ novel.

**Available wherever books are sold, including most
bookstores, supermarkets, drugstores and discount stores.**

Coupon expires December 1, 2006. Redeemable at participating
retail outlets in Canada only. Limit one coupon per customer.

RETAILER: Harlequin Enterprises Limited will pay the face value of this coupon
plus 10.25 cents if submitted by the customer for this specified product only. Any
other use constitutes fraud. Coupon is nonassignable. Void if taxed, prohibited or
restricted by law. Consumer must pay any government taxes. Mail to Harlequin
Enterprises Ltd., P.O. Box 3000, Saint John, New Brunswick E2L 4L3, Canada. Limit
one coupon per customer. Valid in Canada only.

52607136

SNCOUPCDN

Introducing…

nocturne

a spine-tingling new line from Silhouette Books.

These paranormal romances will
seduce you with dark, passionate tales
that stretch the boundaries of conflict,
desire, and life and death, weaving
a tapestry of sensual thrills and chills!

Don't miss the first book…

UNFORGIVEN

by *USA TODAY* bestselling author

LINDSAY McKENNA

Launching October 2006,
wherever books are sold.

If you enjoyed what you just read,
then we've got an offer you can't resist!

Take 2 bestselling love stories FREE!

Plus get a FREE surprise gift!

COMING NEXT MONTH

#1753 FORBIDDEN MERGER—Emilie Rose
The Elliotts
When a business tycoon falls for the one woman he can't have,
their secret affair threatens to stir up *more* than a few hot nights.

#1754 BLACKHAWK'S BETRAYAL—Barbara McCauley
Secrets!
Mixing business with pleasure was not on her agenda…but
bedding the boss may be the key to discovering the truth about her
family.

#1755 THE PART-TIME WIFE—Maureen Child
Secret Lives of Society Wives
A society wife learns her husband is leading a double life and gets
whisked into his world of scandals and secrets.

#1756 THE MORNING-AFTER PROPOSAL—
Sheri WhiteFeather
The Trueno Brides
He vowed to protect her under one condition—she become his
wife. Will she succumb to her desires and his zealous proposal?

#1757 REVENGE OF THE SECOND SON—Sara Orwig
The Wealthy Ransomes
This billionaire bets he can seduce his rival's stunning
granddaughter, until the tables turn and *she* raises the stakes.

#1758 THE BOSS'S CHRISTMAS SEDUCTION—
Yvonne Lindsay
Sleeping with the boss she secretly loved was not the best career
move. Now she had to tell him she was expecting his baby.

SDCNM0906